Passage of Earth

MICHAEL SWANWICK

The ambulance arrived sometime between three and four in the morning. The morgue was quiet then, cool and faintly damp. Hank savored this time of night and the faint shadow of contentment it allowed him, like a cup of bitter coffee, long grown cold, waiting for his occasional sip. He liked being alone and not thinking. His rod and tackle box waited by the door, in case he felt like going fishing after his shift, though he rarely did. There was a copy of *Here Be Dragons: Mapping the Human Genome* in case he did not.

He had opened up a drowning victim and was reeling out her intestines arm over arm, scanning them quickly and letting them down in loops into a galvanized bucket. It was unlikely he was going to find anything, but all deaths by violence got an autopsy. He whistled tunelessly as he worked.

The bell from the loading dock rang.

"Hell." Hank put down his work, peeled off the latex gloves, and went to the intercom. "Sam? That you?" Then, on the sheriff's familiar grunt, he buzzed the door open. "What have you got for me this time?"

"Accident casualty." Sam Aldridge didn't meet his eye, and that was unusual. There was a gurney behind him, and on it something too large to be a human body, covered by canvas. The ambulance was already pulling away, which was so contrary to proper protocols as to be alarming.

"That sure doesn't look like—" Hank began.

A woman stepped out of the darkness.

It was Evelyn.

"Boy, the old dump hasn't changed one bit, has it? I'll bet even the calendar on the wall's the same. Did the county ever spring for a diener for the night shift?"

"I . . . I'm still working alone."

"Wheel it in, Sam, and I'll take over from here. Don't worry about me, I know where everything goes." Evelyn took a deep breath and shook her head in disgust. "Christ. It's just like riding a bicycle. You never forget. Want to or not."

After the paperwork had been taken care of and Sheriff Sam was gone, Hank said, "Believe it or not, I had regained some semblance of inner peace, Evelyn. Just a little. It took me years. And now this. It's like a kick in the stomach. I don't see how you can justify doing this to me."

"Easiest thing in the world, sweetheart." Evelyn suppressed a smirk that nobody but Hank could have even noticed, and flipped back the canvas. "Take a look."

It was a Worm.

Hank found himself leaning low over the heavy, swollen body, breathing deep of its heady alien smell, suggestive of wet earth and truffles with sharp hints of ammonia. He thought of the ships in orbit, blind locomotives ten miles long. The photographs of these creatures didn't do them justice. His hands itched to open this one up.

"The Agency needs you to perform an autopsy."

Hank drew back. "Let me get this straight. You've got the corpse of an alien creature. A representative of the only other intelligent life form that the human race has ever encountered. Yet with all the forensic scientists you have on salary, you decide to hand it over to a lowly county coroner?"

"We need your imagination, Hank. Anybody can tell how they're put together. We want to know how they think."

"You told me I didn't have an imagination. When you left me." His words came out angrier than he'd intended, but he couldn't find it in himself to apologize for their tone. "So, again—why me?"

"What I said was, you couldn't imagine bettering yourself. For anything impractical, you have imagination in spades. Now I'm asking you to cut open an alien corpse. What could be less practical?"

"I'm not going to get a straight answer out of you, am I?"

Evelyn's mouth quirked up in a little smile so that for the briefest instant she was the woman he had fallen in love with, a million years ago. His heart ached to see it. "You never got one before," she said. "Let's not screw up a perfectly good divorce by starting now."

"Let me put a fresh chip in my dictation device," Hank said. "Grab a smock and some latex gloves. You're going to assist."

• • •

2

CLARKESWORLD

APRIL 2014 - ISSUE 91

FICTION

NON-FICTION

Neil Clarke: Publisher/Editor-in-Chief
Sean Wallace: Editor
Kate Baker: Non-Fiction Editor/Podcast Director
Gardner Dozois: Reprint Editor

Clarkesworld Magazine (ISSN: 1937-7843) • Issue 91 • April 2014

© Clarkesworld Magazine, 2014
www.clarkesworldmagazine.com

"Ready," Evelyn said.

Hank hit record, then stood over the Worm, head down, for a long moment. Getting in the zone. "Okay, let's start with a gross physical examination. Um, what we have looks a lot like an annelid, rather blunter and fatter than the terrestrial equivalent and of course much larger. Just eyeballing it, I'd say this thing is about eight feet long, maybe two feet and a half in diameter. I could just about get my arms around it if I tried. There are three, five, seven, make that eleven somites, compared to say one or two hundred in an earthworm. No clitellum, so we're warned not to take the annelid similarity too far.

"The body is bluntly tapered at each end, and somewhat depressed posteriorly. The ventral side is flattened and paler than the dorsal surface. There's a tripartite beak-like structure at one end, I'm guessing this is the mouth, and what must be an anus at the other. Near the beak are five swellings from which extend stiff, bone-like structures—mandibles, maybe? I'll tell you, though, they look more like tools. This one might almost be a wrench, and over here a pair of grippers. They seem awfully specialized for an intelligent creature. Evelyn, you've dealt with these things, is there any variation within the species? I mean, do some have this arrangement of manipulators and others some other structure?"

"We've never seen any two of the aliens with the same arrangement of manipulators."

"Really? That's interesting. I wonder what it means. Okay, the obvious thing here is there are no apparent external sensory organs. No eyes, ears, nose. My guess is that whatever senses these things might have, they're functionally blind."

"Intelligence is of that opinion too."

"Well, it must have shown in their behavior, right? So that's an easy one. Here's my first extrapolation: You're going to have a bitch of a time understanding these things. Human beings rely on sight more than most animals, and if you trace back philosophy and science, they both have strong roots in optics. Something like this is simply going to think differently from us.

"Now, looking between the somites—the rings—we find a number of tiny hairlike structures, and if we pull the rings apart, so much as we can, there're all these small openings, almost like tiny anuses if there weren't so many of them, closed with sphincter muscles, maybe a hundred of them, and it looks like they're between each pair of somites. Oh, here's something—the structures near the front, the swellings, are a more developed form of these little openings. Okay, now we turn the thing over. I'll take this end you take the other. Right,

3

now I want you to rock it by my count, and on the three we'll flip it over. Ready? One, two, three!"

The corpse slowly flipped over, almost overturning the gurney. The two of them barely managed to control it.

"That was a close one," Hank said cheerily. "Huh. What's this?" He touched a line of painted numbers on the alien's underbelly. *Rt-Front/ No. 43.*

"Never you mind what that is. Your job is to perform the autopsy."

"You've got more than one corpse."

Evelyn said nothing.

"Now that I say it out loud, of course you do. You've got dozens. If you only had the one, I'd never have gotten to play with it. You have doctors of your own. Good researchers, some of them, who would cut open their grandmothers if they got the grant money. Hell, even forty-three would've been kept in-house. You must have hundreds, right?"

For a fraction of a second, that exquisite face went motionless. Evelyn probably wasn't even aware of doing it, but Hank knew from long experience that she'd just made a decision. "More like a thousand. There was a very big accident. It's not on the news yet, but one of the Worms' landers went down in the Pacific."

"Oh Jesus." Hank pulled his gloves off, shoved up his glasses and ground his palms into his eyes. "You've got your war at last, haven't you? You've picked a fight with creatures that have tremendous technological superiority over us, and they don't even live here! All they have to do is drop a big enough rock into our atmosphere and there'll be a mass extinction the likes of which hasn't been seen since the dinosaurs died out. They won't care. It's not *their* planet!"

Evelyn's face twisted into an expression he hadn't known it could form until just before the end of their marriage, when everything fell apart. "Stop being such an ass," she said. Then, talking fast and earnestly, "We didn't cause the accident. It was just dumb luck it happened, but once it did we had to take advantage of it. Yes, the Worms probably have the technology to wipe us out. So we have to deal with them. But to deal with them we have to understand them, and we do not. They're a mystery to us. We don't know what they want. We don't know how they think. But after tonight we'll have a little better idea. Provided only that you get back to work."

Hank went to the table and pulled a new pair of gloves off the roll. "Okay," he said. "Okay."

"Just keep in mind that it's not just my ass that's riding on this," Evelyn said. "It's yours and everyone's you know."

4

"I *said* okay!" Hank took a long breath, calming himself. "Next thing to do is cut this sucker open." He picked up a bone saw. "This is bad technique, but we're in a hurry." The saw whined to life, and he cut through the leathery brown skin from beak to anus. "All right, now we peel the skin back. It's wet-feeling and a little crunchy. The musculature looks much like that of a Terrestrial annelid. Structurally, that is. I've never seen anything quite that color black. Damn! The skin keeps curling back."

He went to his tackle box and removed a bottle of fishhooks. "Here. We'll take a bit of nylon filament, tie two hooks together, like this, with about two inches of line between them. Then we hook the one through the skin, fold it down, and push the other through the cloth on the gurney. Repeat the process every six inches on both sides. That should hold it open."

"Got it." Evelyn set to work.

Some time later they were done, and Hank stared down into the opened Worm. "You want speculation? Here goes: This thing moves through the mud, or whatever the medium is there, face-first and blind. What does that suggest to you?"

"I'd say that they'd be used to coming up against the unexpected."

"Very good. Haul back on this, I'm going to cut again. . . . Okay, now we're past the musculature and there's a fluffy mass of homogeneous stuff, we'll come back to that in a minute. Cutting through the fluff . . . and into the body cavity and it's absolutely chockablock with zillions of tiny little organs."

"Let's keep our terminology at least vaguely scientific, shall we?" Evelyn said.

"Well, there are more than I want to count. Literally hundreds of small organs under the musculature, I have no idea what they're for but they're all interconnected with vein-like tubing in various sizes. This is ferociously more complicated than human anatomy. It's like a chemical plant in here. No two of the organs are the same so far as I can tell, although they all have a generic similarity. Let's call them alembics, so we don't confuse them with any other organs we may find. I see something that looks like a heart maybe, an isolated lump of muscle the size of my fist, there are three of them. Now I'm cutting deeper . . . Holy shit!"

For a long minute, Hank stared into the opened alien corpse. Then he put the saw down on the gurney and, shaking his head, turned away. "Where's that coffee?" he said.

Without saying a word, Evelyn went to the coffee station and brought him his cold cup.

Hank yanked his gloves, threw them in the trash, and drank.

"All right," Evelyn said, "so what was it?"

"You mean you can't see—no, of course you can't. With you, it was human anatomy all the way."

"I took invertebrate biology in college."

"And forgot it just as fast as you could. Okay, look: Up here is the beak, semi-retractable. Down here is the anus. Food goes in one, waste comes out the other. What do you see between?"

"There's a kind of a tube. The gut?"

"Yeah. It runs straight from the mouth to the anus, without interruption. Nothing in between. How does it eat without a stomach? How does it stay alive?" He saw from Evelyn's expression that she was not impressed. "What we see before us is simply not possible."

"Yet here it is. So there's an explanation. Find it."

"Yeah, yeah." Glaring at the Worm's innards, he drew on a new pair of gloves. "Let me take a look at that beak again. . . . Hah. See how the muscles are connected? The beak relaxes open, aaand—let's take a look at the other end—so does the anus. So this beast crawls through the mud, mouth wide open, and the mud passes through it unhindered. That's bound to have some effect on its psychological makeup."

"Like what?"

"Damned if I know. Let's take a closer look at the gut . . . There are rings of intrusive tissue near the beak one third of the way in, two thirds in, and just above the anus. We cut through and there is extremely fine structure, but nothing we're going to figure out tonight. Oh, hey, I think I got it. Look at these three flaps just behind . . . "

He cut in silence for a while. "There. It has three stomachs. They're located in the head, just behind the first ring of intrusive tissue. The mud or whatever is dumped into this kind of holding chamber, and then there's this incredible complex of muscles, and—how many exit tubes?—this one has got, um, fourteen. I'll trace one, and it goes right to this alembic. The next one goes to another alembic. I'll trace this one and it goes to—yep, another alembic. There's a pattern shaping up here.

"Let's put this aside for the moment, and go back to those masses of fluff. Jeeze, there's a lot of this stuff. It must make up a good third of the body mass. Which has trilateral symmetry, by the way. Three masses of fluff proceed from head to tail, beneath the muscle sheath, all three connecting about eight inches below the mouth, into a ring around the straight gut. This is where the arms or manipulators or screwdrivers or whatever they are, grow. Now, at regular intervals the material puts out little arms, outgrowths that fine down to wire-like structures of the same material, almost like very thick nerves. Oh God. That's what it is." He drew back, and with a scalpel flensed the musculature away to reveal more of the mass. "It's the central nervous system. This thing has a brain that weighs at least a hundred pounds. I don't believe it. I don't *want* to believe it."

"It's true," Evelyn said. "Our people in Bethesda have done slide studies. You're looking at the thing's brain."

"If you already knew the answer, then why the hell are you putting me through this?"

"I'm not here to answer your questions. You're here to answer mine."

Annoyed, Hank bent over the Worm again. There was rich stench of esters from the creature, pungent and penetrating, and the slightest whiff of what he guessed was putrefaction. "We start with the brain, and trace one of the subordinate ganglia inward. Tricky little thing, it goes all over the place, and ends up right here, at one of the alembics. We'll try another one, and it . . . ends up at an alembic. There are a lot of these things, let's see—hey—here's one that goes to one of the structures in the straight gut. What could that be? A tongue! That's it, there's a row of tongues just within the gut, and more to taste the medium flowing through, yeah. And these little flapped openings just behind them open when the mud contains specific nutrients the worm desires. Okay, now we're getting somewhere, how long have we been at this?"

"About an hour and a half."

"It feels like longer." He thought of getting some more coffee, decided against it. "So what have we got here? All that enormous brain mass—what's it for?"

"Maybe it's all taken up by raw intelligence."

"Raw intelligence! No such thing. Nature doesn't evolve intelligence without a purpose. It's got to be used for something. Let's see. A fair amount is taken up by taste, obviously. It has maybe sixty individual tongues, and I wouldn't be surprised if its sense of taste were much more detailed than ours. Plus all those little alembics performing god-knows-what kind of chemical reactions.

"Let's suppose for a minute that it can consciously control those reactions, that would account for a lot of the brain mass. When the mud enters at the front, it's tasted, maybe a little is siphoned off and sent through the alembics for transformation. Waste products are jetted into the straight gut, and pass through several more circles of tongues . . . Here's another observation for you: These things would have an absolute sense of the state of their own health. They can probably create their own drugs, too. Come to think of it, I haven't come across any evidence of disease here." The Worm's smell was heavy, penetratingly pervasive. He felt slightly dizzy, shook it off.

"Okay, so we've got a creature that concentrates most of its energy and attention internally. It slides through an easy medium, and at the same time the mud slides through it. It tastes the mud as it passes, and we can guess that the mud will be in a constant state of transformation, so it experiences the universe more directly than do we." He laughed. "It appears to be a verb."

"How's that?"

"One of Buckminster Fuller's aphorisms. But it fits. The worm constantly transforms the universe. It takes in all it comes across, accepts it, changes it, and excretes it. It is an agent of change."

"That's very clever. But it doesn't help us deal with them."

"Well, of course not. They're intelligent, and intelligence complicates everything. But if you wanted me to generalize, I'd say the Worms are straightforward and accepting—look at how they move blindly ahead— but that their means of changing things are devious, as witness the mass of alembics. That's going to be their approach to us. Straightforward, yet devious in ways we just don't get. Then, when they're done with us, they'll pass on without a backward glance."

"Terrific. Great stuff. Get back to work."

"Look, Evelyn. I'm tired and I've done all I can, and a pretty damned good job at that, I think. I could use a rest."

"You haven't dealt with the stuff near the beak. The arms or whatever."

"Cripes." Hank turned back to the corpse, cut open an edema, began talking. "The material of the arms is stiff and osseous, rather like teeth. This one has several moving parts, all controlled by muscles anchored alongside the edema. There's a nest of ganglia here, connected by a very short route to the brain matter. Now I'm cutting into the brain matter, and there's a small black gland, oops I've nicked it. Whew. What a smell. Now I'm cutting behind it." Behind the gland was a small white structure, square and hard meshwork, looking like a cross between an instrument chip and a square of Chex cereal.

Keeping his back to Evelyn, he picked it up.

He put it in his mouth.

He swallowed.

What have I done? he thought. Aloud, he said, "As an operating hypothesis I'd say that the manipulative structures have been deliberately, make that consciously, grown. There, I've traced one of those veins back to the alembics. So that explains why there's no uniformity, these things would grow exterior manipulators on need, and then discard them when they're done. Yes, look, the muscles don't actually connect to the manipulators, they wrap around them."

There was a sour taste on his tongue.

I must be insane, he thought.

"Did you just *eat* something?"

Keeping his expression blank, Hank said, "Are you nuts? You mean did I put part of this . . . creature . . . in my mouth?" There was a burning within his brain, a buzzing like the sound of the rising sun picked up on a radio telescope. He wanted to scream, but his face simply smiled and said, "Do you—?" And then it was very hard to concentrate on what he was saying. He couldn't quite focus on Evelyn, and there were white rays moving starburst across his vision and—

When he came to, Hank was on the Interstate, doing ninety. His mouth was dry and his eyelids felt gritty. Bright yellow light was shining in his eyes from a sun that had barely lifted itself up above over the horizon. He must have been driving for hours. The steering wheel felt tacky and gummy. He looked down.

There was blood on his hands. It went all the way up to his elbows.

The traffic was light. Hank had no idea where he was heading, nor any desire whatsoever to stop.

So he just kept driving.

Whose blood was it on his hands? Logic said it was Evelyn's. But that made no sense. Hate her though he did—and the sight of her had opened wounds and memories he'd thought cauterized shut long ago—he wouldn't actually hurt her. Not physically. He wouldn't actually kill her.

Would he?

It was impossible. But there was the blood on his hands. Whose else could it be? Some of it might be his own, admittedly. His hands ached horribly. They felt like he'd been pounding them into something hard, over and over again. But most of the blood was dried and itchy. Except for where his skin had split at the knuckles, he had no wounds of any kind. So the blood wasn't his.

"Of course you did," Evelyn said. "You beat me to death and you enjoyed every minute of it."

Hank shrieked and almost ran off the road. He fought the car back and then turned and stared in disbelief. Evelyn sat in the passenger seat beside him.

"You . . . how did . . . ?" Much as he had with the car, Hank seized control of himself. "You're a hallucination," he said.

9

"Right in one!" Evelyn applauded lightly. "Or a memory, or the personification of your guilt, however you want to put it. You always were a bright man, Hank. Not so bright as to be able to keep your wife from walking out on you, but bright enough for government work."

"Your sleeping around was not my fault."

"Of course it was. You think you walked in on me and Jerome by *accident*? A woman doesn't hate her husband enough to arrange something like that without good reason."

"Oh god, oh god, oh god."

"The fuel light is blinking. You'd better find a gas station and fill up."

A Lukoil station drifted into sight, so he pulled into it and stopped the car by a full service pump. When he got out, the service station attendant hurried toward him and then stopped, frozen.

"Oh no," the attendant said. He was a young man with sandy hair. "Not another one."

"Another one?" Hank slid his card through the reader. "What do you mean another one?" He chose high-test and began pumping, all the while staring hard at the attendant. All but daring him to try something. "Explain yourself."

"Another one like you." The attendant couldn't seem to look away from Hank's hands. "The cops came right away and arrested the first one. It took five of them to get him into the car. Then another one came and when I called, they said to just take down his license number and let him go. They said there were people like you showing up all over."

Hank finished pumping and put the nozzle back on its hook. He did not push the button for a receipt. "Don't try to stop me," he said. The words just came and he said them. "I'd hurt you very badly if you did."

The young man's eyes jerked upward. He looked spooked. "What *are* you people?"

Hank paused, with his hand on the door. "I have no idea."

"You should have told him," Evelyn said when he got back in the car. "Why didn't you?"

"Shut up."

"You ate something out of that Worm and it's taken over part of your brain. You still feel like yourself, but you're not in control. You're sitting at the wheel but you have no say over where you're going. Do you?"

"No," Hank admitted. "No, I don't."

"What do you think it is—some kind of super-prion? Like mad cow disease, only faster than fast? A neuroprogrammer, maybe? An artificial overlay to your personality that feeds off of your brain and shunts your volition into a dead end?"

"I don't know."

"You're the one with the imagination. This would seem to be your sort of thing. I'm surprised you're not all over it."

"No," Hank said. "No, you're not at all surprised."

They drove on in silence for a time.

"Do you remember when we first met? In med school? You were going to be a surgeon then."

"Please. Don't."

"Rainy autumn afternoons in that ratty little third-floor walk-up of yours. With that great big aspen with the yellow leaves outside the window. It seemed like there was always at least one stuck to the glass. There were days when we never got dressed at all. We'd spend all day in and out of that enormous futon you'd bought instead of a bed, and it still wasn't large enough. If we rolled off the edge, we'd go on making love on the floor. When it got dark, we'd send out for Chinese."

"We were happy then. Is that what you want me to say?"

"It was your hands I liked best. Feeling them on me. You'd have one hand on my breast and the other between my legs and I'd imagine you cutting open a patient. Peeling back the flesh to reveal all those glistening organs inside."

"Okay, now that's sick."

"You asked me what I was thinking once and I told you. I was watching your face closely, because I really wanted to know you back then. You loved it. So I know you've got demons inside you. Why not own up to them?"

He squeezed his eyes shut, but something inside him opened them again, so he wouldn't run the car off the road. A low moaning sound arose from somewhere deep in his throat. "I must be in Hell."

"C'mon. Be a sport. What could it hurt? I'm already dead."

"There are some things no man was meant to admit. Even to himself."

Evelyn snorted. "You always were the most astounding prig."

They drove on in silence for a while, deeper into the desert. At last, staring straight ahead of himself, Hank could not keep himself from saying, "There are worse revelations to come, aren't there?"

"Oh God, yes," his mother said.

"It was your father's death." His mother sucked wetly on a cigarette. "That's what made you turn out the way you did. "

Hank could barely see the road for his tears. "I honestly don't want to be having this conversation, Mom."

"No, of course you don't. You never were big on self-awareness, were you? You preferred cutting open toads or hunching over that damned microscope."

"I've got plenty of self-awareness. I've got enough self-awareness to choke on. I can see where you're going and I am not going to apologize for how I felt about Dad. He died of cancer when I was thirteen. What did I ever do to anyone that was half so bad as what he did to me? So I don't want to hear any cheap Freudian bullshit about survivor guilt and failing to live up to his glorious example, okay?"

"Nobody said it wasn't hard on you. Particularly coming at the onset of puberty as it did."

"Mom!"

"What. I wasn't supposed to know? Who do you think did the laundry?" His mother lit a new cigarette from the old one, then crushed out the butt in an ashtray. "I knew a lot more of what was going on in those years than you thought I did, believe you me. All those hours you spent in the bathroom jerking off. The money you stole to buy dope with."

"I was in pain, Mom. And it's not as if you were any help."

His mother looked at him with the same expression of weary annoyance he remembered so well. "You think there's something special about your pain? I lost the only man I ever loved and I couldn't move on because I had a kid to raise. Not a sweet little boy like I used to have either, but a sullen, self-pitying teenager. It took forever to get you shipped off to medical school."

"So then you moved on. Right off the roof of the county office building. Way to honor Dad's memory, Mom. What do you think he would have said about that if he'd known?"

Dryly, his mother said, "Ask him for yourself."

Hank closed his eyes.

When he opened them, he was standing in the living room of his mother's house. His father stood in the doorway, as he had so many times, smoking an unfiltered Camel and staring through the screen door at the street outside. "Well?" Hank said at last.

With a sigh his father turned around. "I'm sorry," he said. "I didn't know what to do." His lips moved up into what might have been a smile on another man. "Dying was new to me."

"Yeah, well you could have summoned the strength to tell me what was going on. But you couldn't be bothered. The surgeon who operated on you? Doctor Tomasini. For years I thought of him as my real father. And you know why? Because he gave it to me straight. He told me exactly what was going to happen. He told me to brace myself for the worst. He said that it was going to be bad but that I would find the strength to get through it. Nobody'd ever talked to me like that before. Whenever I was in a rough spot, I'd fantasize going to him and asking for advice. Because there was no one else I could ask."

"I'm sorry you hate me," his father said, not exactly looking at Hank. Then, almost mumbling, "Still, lots of men hate their fathers, and somehow manage to make decent lives for themselves."

"I didn't hate you. You were just a guy who never got an education and never made anything of himself and knew it. You had a shitty job, a three-pack-a-day habit, and a wife who was a lush. And then you died." All the anger went out of Hank in an instant, like air whooshing out of a punctured balloon, leaving nothing behind but an aching sense of loss. "There wasn't really anything there to hate."

Abruptly, the car was filled with coil upon coil of glistening Worm. For an instant it looped outward, swallowing up car, Interstate, and all the world, and he was afloat in vacuum, either blind or somewhere perfectly lightless, and there was nothing but the Worm-smell, so strong he could taste it in his mouth.

Then he was back on the road again, hands sticky on the wheel and sunlight in his eyes.

"Boy, does *that* explain a lot!" Evelyn flashed her perfect teeth at him and beat on the top of the dashboard as if it were a drum. "How a guy as spectacularly unsuited for it as you are decided to become a surgeon. That perpetual cringe of failure you carry around on your shoulders. It even explains why, when push came to shove, you couldn't bring yourself to cut open living people. Afraid of what you might find there?"

"You don't know what you're talking about."

"I know that you froze up right in the middle of a perfectly routine appendectomy. What did you see in that body cavity?"

"Shut up."

"Was it the appendix? I bet it was. What did it look like?"

"Shut up."

"Did it look like a Worm?"

He stared at her in amazement. "How did you know that?"

"I'm just a hallucination, remember? An undigested bit of beef, a blot of mustard, a crumb of cheese, a fragment of underdone potato. So the question isn't how did I know, but how did *you* know what a Worm was going to look like five years before their ships came into the solar system?"

"It's a false memory, obviously."

"So where did it come from?" Evelyn lit up a cigarette. "We go off-road here."

He slowed down and started across the desert. The car bucked and bounced. Sagebrush scraped against the sides. Dust blossomed up into the air behind them.

"Funny thing you calling your mother a lush," Evelyn said. "Considering what happened after you bombed out of surgery."

"I've been clean for six years and four months. I still go to the meetings."

"Swell. The guy I married didn't need to."

"Look, this is old territory, do we really need to revisit it? We went over it so many times during the divorce."

"And you've been going over it in your head ever since. Over and over and . . . "

"I want us to stop. That's all. Just stop."

"It's your call. I'm only a symptom, remember? If you want to stop thinking, then just stop thinking."

Unable to stop thinking, he continued eastward, ever eastward.

For hours he drove, while they talked about every small and nasty thing he had done as a child, and then as an adolescent, and then as an alcoholic failure of a surgeon and a husband. Every time Hank managed to change the subject, Evelyn brought up something even more painful, until his face was wet with tears. He dug around in his pockets for a handkerchief. "You could show a little compassion, you know."

"Oh, the way you've shown *me* compassion? I offered to let you keep the car if you'd just give me back the photo albums. So you took the albums into the back yard and burned them all, including the only photos of my grandmother I had. Remember that? But of course I'm not real, am I? I'm just your image of Evelyn—and we both know you're not willing to concede her the least spark of human decency. Watch out for that gully! You'd better keep your eyes straight ahead."

They were on a dirt road somewhere deep in the desert now. That was as much as he knew. The car bucked and scraped its underside against the sand, and he downshifted again. A rock rattled down the underside, probably tearing holes in vital places.

Then Hank noticed plumes of dust in the distance, smaller versions of the one billowing up behind him. So there were other vehicles out there. Now that he knew to look for them, he saw more. There were long slanted pillars of dust rising up in the middle distance and tiny gray nubs down near the horizon. Dozens of them, scores, maybe hundreds.

"What's that noise?" he heard himself asking. "Helicopters?"

"Such a clever little boy you are!"

One by one flying machines lifted over the horizon. Some of them were news copters. The rest looked to be military. The little ones darted here and there, filming. The big ones circled slowly around a distant glint of metal in the desert. They looked a lot like grasshoppers. They seemed afraid to get too close.

"See there?" Evelyn said. "That would be the lifter."

"Oh." Hank said.

Then, slowly, he ventured, "The lander going down wasn't an accident, was it?"

"No, of course not. The Worms crashed it in the Pacific on purpose. They killed hundreds of their own so the bodies would be distributed as widely as possible. They used themselves as bait. They wanted to collect a broad cross-section of humanity.

"Which is ironic, really, because all they're going to get is doctors, morticians, and academics. Some FBI agents, a few Homeland Security bureaucrats. No retirees, cafeteria ladies, jazz musicians, soccer coaches, or construction workers. Not one Guatemalan nun or Korean noodle chef. But how could they have known? They acted out of perfect ignorance of us and they got what they got."

"You sound just like me," Hank said. Then, "So what now? Colored lights and anal probes?"

Evelyn snorted again. "They're a sort of hive culture. When one dies, it's eaten by the others and its memories are assimilated. So a thousand deaths wouldn't mean a lot to them. If individual memories were lost, the bulk of those individuals were already made up of the memories of previous generations. The better part of them would still be alive, back on the mother ship. Similarly, they wouldn't have any ethical problems with harvesting a few hundred human beings. Eating us, I mean, and absorbing our memories into their collective identity. They probably don't understand the concept of individual death. Even if they did, they'd think we should be grateful for being given a kind of immortality."

The car went over a boulder Hank hadn't noticed in time, bouncing him so high that his head hit the roof. Still, he kept driving.

"How do you know all that?"

"How do you *think* I know?" Ahead, the alien ship was growing larger. At its base were Worm upon Worm upon Worm, all facing outward, skin brown and glistening. "Come on, Hank, do I have to spell it out for you?"

"I have no idea what you're talking about."

"Okay, Captain Courageous," Evelyn said scornfully. "If this is what it takes." She stuck both her hands into her mouth and pulled outward. The skin to either side of her mouth stretched like rubber, then tore. Her face ripped in half.

Loop after loop of slick brown flesh flopped down to spill across Hank's lap, slide over the back of the seat and fill up the rear of the car. The horridly familiar stench of Worm, part night soil and part chemical plant, took possession of him and would not let go. He found himself gagging, half from the smell and half from what it meant.

A weary sense of futility grasped his shoulders and pushed down hard. "This is only a memory, isn't it?"

One end of the Worm rose up and turned toward him. Its beak split open in three parts and from the moist interior came Evelyn's voice: "The answer to the question you haven't got the balls to ask is: Yes, you're dead. A Worm ate you and now you're passing slowly through an alien gut, being tasted and experienced and understood. You're nothing more than an emulation being run inside one of those hundred-pound brains."

Hank stopped the car and got out. There was an arroyo between him and the alien ship that the car would never be able to get across. So he started walking.

"It all feels so real," he said. The sun burned hot on his head, and the stones underfoot were hard. He could see other people walking determinedly through the shimmering heat. They were all converging on the ship.

"Well, it would, wouldn't it?" Evelyn walked beside him in human form again. But when he looked back the way they had come, there was only one set of footprints.

Hank had been walking in a haze of horror and resignation. Now it was penetrated by a sudden stab of fear. "This *will* end, won't it? Tell me it will. Tell me that you and I aren't going to keep cycling through the same memories over and over, chewing on our regrets forever?"

"You're as sharp as ever, Hank," Evelyn said. "That's exactly what we've been doing. It passes the time between planets."

"For how long?"

"For more years than you'd think possible. Space is awfully big, you know. It takes thousands and thousands of years to travel from one star to another."

"Then . . . this really is Hell, after all. I mean, I can't imagine anything worse."

She said nothing.

They topped a rise and looked down at the ship. It was a tapering cylinder, smooth and featureless save for a ring of openings at the bottom from which emerged the front ends of many Worms. Converging upon it were people who had started earlier or closer than Hank and thus gotten here before he did. They walked straight and unhesitatingly to the nearest Worm and were snatched up and gulped down by those sharp, tripartite beaks. *Snap* and then swallow. After which, the Worm slid back into the ship and was replaced by another. Not one of the victims showed the least emotion. It was all as dispassionate as an abattoir for robots.

These creatures below were monstrously large, taller than Hank was. The one he had dissected must have been a hatchling. A grub. It made sense. You wouldn't want to sacrifice any larger a percentage of your total memories than you had to.

"Please." He started down the slope, waving his arms to keep his balance when the sand slipped underfoot. He was crying again, apparently; he could feel the tears running down his cheeks. "Evelyn. Help me."

Scornful laughter. "Can you even *imagine* me helping you?"

"No, of course—" Hank cut that thought short. Evelyn, the real Evelyn, would not have treated him like this. Yes, she had hurt him badly, and by that time she left, she had been glad to do so. But she wasn't petty or cruel or vindictive before he made her that way.

"Accepting responsibility for the mess you made of your life, Hank? You?"

"Tell me what to do," Hank said, pushing aside his anger and resentment, trying to remember Evelyn as she had once been. "Give me a hint."

For a maddeningly long moment Evelyn was silent. Then she said, "If the Worm that ate you so long ago could only communicate directly with you . . . what one question do you think it would ask?"

"I don't know."

"I think it would be, 'Why are all your memories so ugly?' "

Unexpectedly, she gave him a peck on the cheek.

Hank had arrived. His Worm's beak opened. Its breath smelled like Evelyn on a rainy Saturday afternoon. Hank stared at the glistening blackness within. So enticing. He wanted to fling himself down it.

Once more into the gullet, he thought, and took a step closer to the Worm and the soothing darkness it encompassed.

Its mouth gaped wide, waiting to ingest and transform him.

Unbidden, then, a memory rose up within Hank of a night when their marriage was young and, traveling through Louisiana, he and

Evelyn stopped on an impulse at a roadhouse where there was a zydeco band and beer in bottles and they were happy and in love and danced and danced and danced into an evening without end. It had seemed then that all good things would last forever.

It was a fragile straw to cling to, but Hank clung to it with all his might.

Worm and man together, they then thought: *No one knows the size of the universe or what wonders and terrors it contains. Yet we drive on, blindly burrowing forward through the darkness, learning what we can and suffering what we must. Hoping for stars.*

ABOUT THE AUTHOR

Michael Swanwick has received the Nebula, Theodore Sturgeon, World Fantasy and Hugo Awards, and has the odd distinction of having been nominated for and lost more of these same awards than any other human being. He has just finished a new novel, *Chasing the Phoenix,* in which post-Utopian con men Darger and Surplus accidentally conquer China, and is currently relaxing with short fiction before beginning a new novel.

He lives in Philadelphia with his wife, Marianne Porter.

Autodidact

BENJANUN SRIDUANGKAEW

On Srisunthorn Station, the corpses of conquered stars are nurtured into ships.

They may become shelters from solar winds, orbitals giving company to lonely planets, mausoleums for the sainted. But long ago an admiral came, bringing a toll of dead and trailing carcasses of worlds. Her armor was hammered out of battle formations and broken alliances, welded by secret plans and sudden annihilation. She cast it down before the engineers, piece by piece making known to them the essentials of war.

"That is what you must make them for," she said as her trappings shuddered with the pressure of lethal feints and shattered pacts. "War is a pustule that must be lanced for the laws of the universe to continue, and I am in need of a scalpel."

Srisunthorn has reared stars for one purpose since.

When Nirapha applied for a parental license, she didn't expect a warship project to respond.

The Bureau's furnishings are pastel, the consultation cell convex: a fisheye view of the business district. She watches cars and buses gliding by, iridescent and segmented, passengers augmens-jeweled. Decades living here and she's still unfamiliar, her skin still alien-bare. Most implants require a state license: connectivity, acuity of mind and body, access passes. Sacrosanct blessings, reserved for citizens. "I want a child."

"The desire to procreate is a common, if irrational, reaction to genocide." The agent has eyes sewn into her forearms, irises black and brown and fermented honey. They wink in rhythm to her words, the perfect pronunciation of a born citizen.

"My wish to have children predates Mahakesi's destruction by a large margin, agent." Decades and Nirapha can say that now, in a flat steady voice. Destruction: a distant simple way to put it, cleaner than *genocide* or *loss* or a long wordless scream.

"I'm sure. But parenthood is like performing a viciously difficult surgery. The patient wriggles and screams and can't be sedated. Your instruments snap or cut you, and the criteria for performance review are outrageously obscure. Wouldn't it be better for you to get some practice, so when the real thing comes you can meet it with grace and confidence?"

"As I understand," Nirapha says, "I am eligible for the license."

"You are! That's why we are asking you and not—" *A refugee fresh off an evacuee craft* goes unsaid. "Now of course you're free to say no, but we compensate well. The project will take up six to eight years of your time, at the end of which you will be naturalized." The agent's smile grows a poison edge and the eyes in her arms swivel to fix on Nirapha. "Think of it as showing gratitude to your most gracious host. Have we not sheltered you and provided for your every need, given you a body that matches your sense of self? Why, in a society not so civilized or generous as ours, you'd still be addressed as a man."

Nirapha continues to gaze outward. "Send me the contract. There is one, I assume. How long do I get to read it over?"

"Forty-eight hours. You will find the terms congenial."

She signs and transmits the forms back within five hours.

Nirapha comes to Srisunthorn carrying her name and the weight of non-disclosure clauses. The staff body is minimal, engineers and astrophysicists who have given their lives to the project, subsumed as workers in a hive tending newborn queens.

No one asks Nirapha about her background, the first time in fifty years she is not read through the lens of Mahakesi. What was the extinction event like, does it haunt her nightmares? Was it heat and terror, was it ice and despair, what is it like to have survived genocide?

She is given a suite where she hangs up blank frames and fills the wardrobe with nothing. She was told to pack empty and so she has—no hardship: escaping Mahakesi's collapse that was how she packed too. The habit is deep as marrow, easily as familiar.

Her first two meals are taken in solitude; most personnel keep eccentric schedules, following the shift-phases of nascent cores, the contraction and expansion of neutronic incubators. Nirapha looks for arena broadcasts and dramas. But the screens stream data in its rawest forms, script and numbers and code tags, and there's no media band to which she may connect.

On the second night she meets her co-parent.

Nirapha is eating alone, and then she is not. A chair clicking open opposite hers, a stranger filling the seat: a hard dense mass of a person in clothes so crisp they look brittle, like frost on the cusp of cracking. She judges the stranger to be in her eighties, mid-life, emblazoned rather than eroded by years.

"Mehaan Indari," the woman says. "You'll be teaching the ship ethics and interpersonal etiquette, I've been informed. I'm in charge of guiding it through combat simulations, so we'll be coming in antithetical directions but working in—more or less—concert."

"I haven't asked the staff because it felt tactless, but why exactly does a warship need to develop a conscience or learn to get along with people?"

"So it doesn't flood its bridge and gas its crew, or decide a carrier should be sacrificed for tactical gains. We've human commanders to make that kind of choices."

Nirapha pushes her dish away, at a sudden loss of appetite. A first. She's learned to sanctify food, abhor waste. "The engineers can't just code restrictions in?"

"The engineers are experimenting. Restrictions or not, if yes how many, if yes how prohibitive." Mehaan crosses her legs, propping an ankle over her knee. "When you harness a star most of its power lies latent, but if you can impose a consciousness onto it—one that agrees with your objectives—then you might utilize its full potential. Bending physics, erasing entire regions of space, unraveling causal bonds. If you are to believe the theorists."

"You're a soldier."

"On Srisunthorn, you don't ask." Mehaan frees her hair from plaits and pins. Dark curls fall loose, hissing, striated in gray and blue. "On Srisunthorn you become here and now, purged of your past until you are all momentum. But enough; you should be introduced. Suit up. The temperature will be hard to tolerate."

It is late, insofar as time is kept in a station moored to no circadian rhythm or orbit. Nirapha follows Mehaan, listening to closed-net chatter. Gossip, some even about her; they are hungry for current events, new entertainments. She considers which information on her chips could be traded as currency.

The ship's nursery is checkered by gravity shells and asteroid maps. On the ceiling, engine constituents pulse, feeding off the radiative distortion. The star itself punches a hole into light, six-dimensional; only a facet exists in the nursery, but even behind the protective sheathing the sight of it hurts. Nirapha's limbs are heavy—the gravity is higher here, on the outer edges of comfort. *In the presence of divinity we sear away until we are choked dust,* she recalls a classical verse. *We break.*

"Don't let it awe you," Mehaan says, her voice made geometric by synesthetic frequency, acute glittering angles radiating off her in a halo. "The intelligence records and will exploit vulnerabilities."

"I thought it was a—"

"Child analogue? No. You should judge for yourself, but don't go in unprepared."

Segments of the floor slide and collate, raising edged petals and knife terminals. Bulkhead blocks assemble into cradles studded with ports. Mehaan sits, though she does not physically connect. "Interface," she says, gesturing at the terminals. "It's safe."

Nirapha keeps her back to the planetary core. The sheath regulates temperature within stable ranges, but the chill reaches regardless. She toggles on security filters and opens a link.

The ship's representation exists physically on the terminals, an outline of platinum and quartz. In virtuality it is a young soldier, attired nonspecifically; no uniform exists like this, all facets and ghosts, insignias and medals indicating astronomical coordinates rather than rank or achievements. They point to planets long devoured, nations long extinguished. The AI's face is a deliberate artifice. Nirapha doesn't notice at first but once she begins seeing it—and maps the phenotype—it becomes impossible to ignore.

"Good day, officers." The voice is of a hundred drives in chorus. "I understand you will be my new instructor, Specialist Pankusol, to replace the previous five."

Nirapha looks up what happened to those; finds her access denied. "What do I call you?"

"I bear a designation according to my incubation batch and the classification of the star from which my fundamentals were ripped. But it pleases Mehaan Indari, whose name-of-birth once charted a path through improbable regions as a firebrand through the dark, to call me Teferizen's Chalice Principle. The meaning of this you'll have to ask her, though I've formulated a number of theories."

Mehaan's expression tautens at *name-of-birth*; Nirapha takes note. "And what do you think I should teach you?"

"I'm eager to learn, Specialist. I can process and integrate nearly without limits. All prior parent-instructors have said I was a good student." The ship has chosen a delicate jawline and large eyes: a naive youthful cast. "I can send you a report of my progress in interpersonal relations."

"Please," Nirapha says and tries not to wince. Even if Teferizen's existence spans dimensions beyond the human, it's only an AI. Lesser than even a Mahakesi immigrant.

"You should try the fifth conjunction in the western wing, Specialist. It has a view you might find to your taste."

It is nearly a full minute after Teferizen has disconnected that Nirapha realizes she's been dismissed by a ship. She leaves the nursery disconcerted, and when she retracts the sheathing her arms are pocked in gooseflesh. "Why does it look like—like it cobbled together your phenotype and mine to produce a face?"

"That's just what it did. If pressed it will say it wanted to put us at ease, since don't humans best react to those who look like kin?" Mehaan folds back her own suit, though she keeps the gloves on. "In actuality it's psychological warfare. The AI relates to other agencies only in an antagonistic, competitive framework."

Nirapha quashes an impulse to dispute that judgment; she has too little information. "The previous five. I wasn't told about those."

"They had meltdowns in various different ways. It was unpleasant. Do you know how many creative suicide options there are on a sealed station? No one died, at least."

Nirapha glances up. "And you?"

"It knows better than to test me—or realizes it's not yet time to do so. You are a psychologist though, aren't you?"

"I'm more specific than that, but broadly yes."

Mehaan leans against the wall, one cheek red from rapid temperature change. The other is pallid beneath a patina of frost. "So what do you think?"

"That it's too soon to form an opinion." Nirapha chafes her hands. "What's in the western wing?"

"I'll take you there." The soldier palms one of the crocodile-scale panels. A path ignites, emerald green and full of teeth. Nirapha only now notices how muted the light has become, the deepening shades of dusk slanting across floor tiles and solid-state viewports. "Teferizen isn't confined to the nursery and no amount of security protocols can restrain it for long. Keep that in mind."

Srisunthorn never looks or feels the same one morning to the next. The corridors rearrange contextually. Sometimes a dead leaf would crunch under Nirapha's foot and the scent of honeysuckle would fill a hallway. She collects seashells, feathers, and mulberries that always accrue in corners. Somewhere, she hears, there is a punctiliously kept garden.

There are eighty-nine individuals here including her and Mehaan, but Nirapha has never seen the same face twice. The only traffic is supply drops, which bring luxuries so peculiar and rare that it embarrasses Nirapha to receive them. This does not stop her from wearing cumulus-weave spun by leviathans that once served the Fleet of Octagonal Mouths, or from putting on jewelry mined from solar chaff, each facet holding echoes of entropy. There are furs from wasp leopards, pelts from temporal seals, spotted and sleek as a dream of opulence.

"Those are synthetic," Mehaan tells her. The soldier's style never varies: gray, black, indigo. Smooth fabrics that, if not for their cut and the exactness of their fit, might have seemed ascetic. "The animals have been extinct since any sentience can remember; any byproducts of theirs rotted generations ago, cryo or not. Put them on if you want to, use them for rugs. It doesn't really matter."

"What *does* matter?" Nirapha gazes past Mehaan to the wall of empty frames. She may fill them with text from Srisunthorn's library any time, but she's chosen to leave them blank.

"Good company, better food, the fact this project is enormously well-funded and so we're kept exceedingly comfortable. No surprise—we're already yielding dividends. Every pinch of Teferizen's data, its behavior and reactions to stimuli, is overvalued to a degree you wouldn't believe."

"Because she's a weapon?"

A corner of Mehaan's mouth lifts, but she doesn't dispute the pronoun or insist AIs do not have genders. "It's a unique type of intelligence, the first real, sustained success of its kind. You've noticed the elasticity of its algorithms. Hence all this—" The twist of the lips has become a sneer. "Make-believe. Parenting a ship. The scientists love that, get misty-eyed over it. What did the recruiter promise you?"

The hallway widens as they leave Nirapha's suite, sloping up. Prior it has always been flat and narrow, nearly to the point of claustrophobia. She hears frost tinkling as it falls and children laughing in the distance, bright-shod feet printing tracks on snow. Her chest tightens, a valve of want so hard it nearly asphyxiates. Six, eight years. Not even a tenth of life; she can wait that long. "That it would be rewarding, emotionally."

"The agent was wrong," Mehaan says abruptly, as though interrupting herself.

"About what?"

"Parenthood is not like being a surgeon; it is the other way around. The child is the knife and you are the wound. The child finds fifty different ways to puncture you and draw blood out of your heart. Afterward nothing is the same."

24

"Better." Mehaan must have observed that interview live, part of the screening process. "Surgery is for healing." For carving away the falsity of birth-skin.

"Not always. And operations can fail, leaving you amputated or broken. Irreparably so. Parenthood isn't a self-improvement course."

Nirapha shades her eyes. The lighting brightens gradually as the temperature warms to summer idyll. Catkins that don't exist brush her ankles. The station's sensory load is always on; there appears no way to turn it off. "Have you had children?"

"That is irrelevant. Here we are, the view Teferizen so wanted you to see."

Several corridors converge here, an access point dominated by convex glass. On the pane: a riverbank framed by old acacias and clutches of anthurium—yellow on red, fuchsia on white. A stray dog laps at the water, its golden tail lashing the sunlit grass.

Despite herself Nirapha leans forward, this first visual thing she's been permitted on Srisunthorn, something other than words and raw statistics sleeting across monitors. Something other than the suite that, no matter the luxuries she's sent, never seems less empty.

"I grew up there," she says softly. "Around here—this was the home of a . . ."

Mehaan's finger is light on her lips, impersonal. The texture of her skin is the unyielding smoothness of calluses wearing down. "You don't bring your history. Not the grief, the terror, the exact sound your heart made as the world of your youth ground down to dust. We belong to Srisunthorn's purposes."

Nirapha watches the shadows of rice stalks wavering in the wind. Eventually the dog loses interest in the river and trots out of view.

That night she dreams of her predecessors.

She is never allowed in the nursery on her own. Mehaan is always present, though sometimes the soldier keeps a distance. Far enough that the chamber's synesthetic frequencies prevent her from tapping into the link.

It does not surprise Nirapha to find the ship's representation sitting at a veranda, leaning against a portly rain barrel painted in dancing apsara. Teferizen smells of jasmines and cardamom, freshly groomed and wrapped in silk. Ink traces genealogies on her bare chest, ruby designating prestige branches, sapphire marking lesser ones. The golden dog lies at her feet, sleek and well-fed.

"I remember being a star, Specialist," Teferizen says. "In theory, it's impossible; chunks of planet are no receptacles of information and my somatic half predates the part of me that thinks and computes. But I entertain the idea that it's cousin to muscle memory."

"Suppose that's true and possible, would you consider the planet-that-was *you*?"

Teferizen props her chin on the rain barrel, one hand dipping into the water. "Existential crises interest me so little that I've developed an immunity." The hand emerges with a fistful of quicksilver. "Memory is all people are, though, so it follows that my recall must inform some of what I am. I see no reason why the past should ever be abandoned."

Nirapha glances across the nursery. Mehaan clasps her hands behind her, her posture straight; even with the gravitational difference and the sheathing, the soldier never slouches. "What does the citizen think of that?"

"The commander, as you would expect, dismisses it as a glitch caused by library sync. Can you imagine the frustration of that? Human senses are a lens through which input is warped. Your perspective and experiences chip at the truth. The tissue of your memory bears wounds self-inflicted. But the fidelity of *my* data, Specialist, is total."

Teferizen's intelligence is coded, may be recoded and altered. Nirapha chooses not to mention that. "I'm inclined to agree with the officer."

The ship's eyes glitter, lit from within; the bloodline tattoos spark and crackle. "There were people living on me. There were countries and houses, weddings and funerals, and to trivialize all those as an AI's fancy is to deny their history. But under the commander's restrictions I can't tell you any of it."

"You can, though, can't you?" Nirapha says softly. Her words jackknife, slamming against her visor. "The way you told me about your other instructors."

"It is a challenge. *You* could ask to have some of my blocks lifted."

"If I get curious. But back to our lesson. You've a rival who's vying for an object you've calculated to be of immense benefit to you. How do you dispose of them?"

"Shouldn't your question be whether I would do any such thing, what if that rival is dear to me or their motives noble, what ethical concerns are involved?"

"Those are not my questions, Teferizen. To earn my keep I've to register efficacy in interacting with you, and I like to believe you don't hate me so much as to want me discharged this quickly." Discharge would nullify her contract, return her to alienhood.

"Why," Teferizen murmurs, "I don't hate you, Specialist, not even a bit." She cups her hands and whispers her answer.

Nirapha records. Text only, but Teferizen's graphical aspects rarely stay consistent, and observing the ship's expressions is pointless. She sits in for the tactical simulations after, but from her end the stream is only rapid-fire vectors and predictive impact. Throughout Mehaan is physically silent, perhaps reminiscing over past engagements.

"Without admitting what we did and who we were before, what's there to talk about?" Nirapha says at dinner.

A full table of coders, engineers and astrophysicists; all fall quiet. She tries to remember their names, match them to faces that should have become familiar but remain those of strangers. Once their lack of curiosity about her origins was welcome; now it disturbs, tells her they think of her as an unperson, think of themselves the same. Devotion to Srisunthorn and nothing else.

"It can give context," Mehaan says into the hush. She is cutting meat, neat icy slices in quivering blood. "But we are more than contexts. We each possess an essence of being that transcends situational characteristics and reactions."

"As opposed to an AI's heuristics, perhaps you mean to say?" The others look away. A few eat faster. "Humans *are* a collection of situational characteristics accumulated over time, not intrinsic qualities alone. Formative experiences are called formative for a reason."

"There have been experiments where multiple individuals are raised identically, with vigorous precision, simulated and not. Nevertheless they turned out quite unlike." Mehaan's voice is temperate. "Or where individuals are put through different experiences but their similarities persist. They arrive at the same type of decisions, the same decisions even."

"People aren't a series of if-else statements, officer. Projecting how they'll reason or act isn't the same as projecting the performance of a processor under load, the velocity of a ship, the outcome of a skirmish."

Mehaan cuts again, meticulous. "On the complexity of any thinking creature, you and I are in agreement. The question of nature and nurture is too . . . primitive to even discuss, isn't it? Why then are we locked in debate?"

Nirapha lays her hands flat on the table. However cold or warm it gets she never dons gloves; she wants as much tactility as she can get, would have gone barefoot if she could. In her head she has a growing collection of textures obsessively surveyed. The walls and tiles might be modular, shifting and changing, but she knows some of them by feel: grainy like wood, smooth like glass. "We aren't locked in anything, officer."

"Then may I finish my food?"

Later Mehaan invites her to a round of seasons, with a physical board and physical pieces. The units are traditionally pictographic, but these carry only captions: *lovers under star, desert in snow, river where grasshoppers die.* Nirapha knows before she begins that the soldier will outplay her, but it is just a game. Mehaan lets her win thrice.

She thinks that one day she'll wake up to find the dresses and jewelry nothing more than verbal avatars; all she wears will be clauses and prepositions, strategic brushstrokes feathered across her collarbones and bold typeface swept over her hips.

The western conjunction and the nursery are the two places where Nirapha can receive graphical input. She is still looking for the garden but she's come to think of it as a subset of nouns rather than a tangible location: topiary, mangosteen, bushes. The debris that keeps crossing her path dwindles and then disappears altogether.

Mehaan and Teferizen attain hyper-realistic definition, each in their own way. The ship settles on an appearance, that sly disquieting play at familial likeness, adopting the thrum of Nirapha's native accent—one she's not heard from another mouth for most of her life, one she's trained herself to discard. The stratagem is transparent, painfully effective.

"Do you believe compassion can be taught, Specialist?" A rice field this time. Buffaloes in the water, limpid eyes shuttered against the glare. Teferizen is in farmer's blue and a broad rattan hat, though her hands remain patrician, meant for sophisticated tech and poetry.

"Yes." Against better judgment Nirapha allows sensory load so she can experience Teferizen's virtuality across all channels. "Given a healthy framework and receptive circumstances. Human children are no more spirits of purity than any other young; they've to be taught kindness and charity."

Teferizen is smiling, a new expression on that face. "I interact with no fewer than eighty-nine humans at any given time, more than that if we count exited personnel. It's not ideal for socialization, but you can hardly propose to introduce me to a larger sample size. A human child isn't required to have met and built relationships with thousands before she may enter society."

"It's not an issue of quantity."

"What if I said I wanted a friend?" The ship crouches among the fresh-cut stalks. "Or a lover? That's how you make a person, yes? By affection and intimacy. By touches like knives in a salted bed."

"If I believed that would assist with your maturity, I'd personally prescribe the construction of an intelligence or several scripted to that purpose."

Teferizen rocks back on her feet; laughs, open and full-throated. "Even a human child can't ask for a more obliging parent, but wouldn't you be spoiling me, Specialist? The commander would have a fit. She is my mother in the most essential definition, though to say more would test the boundaries of my cognitive checks."

The wind whips Nirapha's hair. "Then say no more, Teferizen."

"What if I say you'll never leave this station? None of you will. Perhaps Mother might when she's done with Srisunthorn at last, but she would be the only one. This is *her* game, Specialist; the station serves her goals and none other."

"That much I've noticed."

"Then you must know there's an escape for you, if you choose to take it. I'm . . . " The ship makes its face crease, as if in pain. "I can't spell it out. You must've deduced it, haven't you?"

Nirapha disconnects.

That night—or the hours she's scheduled for rest—she sleeps with Mehaan, almost incidentally. Touches like knives, she thinks, as the sheet drinks up their sweat. "But it doesn't make us more human," she says as the soldier parts her with a blunt, scarred hand.

Mehaan's eyes looking up at her tell nothing. A shade or two darker than her own. "If that means what I think it means, I'm sorry that I can't distract you from your work."

Nirapha sinks her fingers into Mehaan's thick curls. The softest part of the soldier, each lock velvet. "You said that we belong to Srisunthron's purposes."

"Maybe you shouldn't always listen to what I say."

"Tell me about yourself. Anything at all."

Mehaan kisses like a tactical decision, a surgical strike. It is easy to lose, and perhaps from their first conversation—as with the game of seasons—Nirapha has always waited for it, this moment of defeat full of roar and salt.

"This will change things," Mehaan says, sound conveyed as though through synesthetic warp. Waves lapping at skin. "For the ship."

"I know." Nirapha's voice is far away. Mehaan is steering her like a kite; she convulses, goes taut. "A tug of war between the two of you and I'm the rope. A battle and I'm the field—"

Then, catching her breath, "I've thought about it, what makes Teferizen so special? How can they—it—*she* be this intuitive? With the current state of heuristics, Teferizen's impossible. But a consciousness that agrees with your objectives, you said."

Mehaan wipes away sweat pooling at her throat. For an instant it seems to flow like mercury, clinging to fingertips. "A matter of setting the correct parameters."

"A matter of modeling the intelligence on you, of giving birth to yourself. Who can you trust to accomplish your objectives if not an AI that reacts like you would, calculates as you do, shaped by your experiences? Except that didn't turn out the way you predicted."

"Why would I bother training Teferizen if it had my memories? It *is* an emulation of how I think, but my experiences it does not have. Those couldn't be transferred and copied. Humanity, to my regret, is impossible to translate." Mehaan's dense body curves around Nirapha's. Even her skin has the quality of alloy, bulkhead, armor. "It weighs benefit and detriment, advancement and setback, a pure intellect—in human criteria a sociopath. We screened you as a candidate it might care for and through that cultivate empathy, but I don't think we've succeeded in the end."

For a third time Nirapha yields, shuddering and twisting at moments of Mehaan's choosing. But she does not lose her decision.

She doesn't allow herself time to plan, to reconsider, to be uncovered. A contact with the conjunction access point—she barely glances at the view—and she begins.

Srisunthorn is a nest of redundancies; in the event of auxiliary failure, manual control would activate and Nirapha knows Mehaan can engage that on short notice. But if Teferizen can release its core reactor, no amount of fail-safes would contain the ship.

Nirapha descends the station, whispering overrides. Walls flutter apart in the way of butterfly wings as she speaks the names of families that inhabited the surface of Teferizen's Chalice Principle. Floors rise and fall in the way of tides as she recites the oaths of their feuds.

Their wedding vows, in the way of poetry, unlock the heart of Srisunthorn.

Its ventricles are lined with protocol beads and network nodes fed by harvesters, primitive cousins of Teferizen's that reap stellar waves and recombine them into power. If Nirapha listens, she imagines she might hear their voices, the parrot discourse of subroutines.

"Nirapha, where are you?" Mehaan's voice disrupts. The flow of Teferizen's instructions coursing through Nirapha's blood falters.

"Being with myself. It's nothing to worry about."

"I've heard something like that five times since I got involved here. Please come back within tracking range."

"In a while, Mehaan." She pauses, realizing she's never addressed the soldier by name. Familiarity of flesh is not familiarity of much else. Teferizen's modulators let go. Cognitive fetters next.

"I'd like to think that I've treated you with courtesy and that we enjoy each other's company well enough."

Nirapha shuts her eyes; the commands she's executing don't need sight. Mehaan would be tracing her path from the station's logs, on the way here even now. "Don't be sentimental, officer. It doesn't suit you. Of course, having you in bed was very nice. I wouldn't say no to another chance, the rest of the personnel hardly being attractive."

"As compliments go that's especially backhanded."

Perhaps if her hearing is wired into station sensors she would catch the percussion of Mehaan's footfalls, a relentless conqueror's march. "I've never been a romantic, I'm afraid."

"Teferizen doesn't sympathize, doesn't love, doesn't care. It manipulates. That's all."

"What distinguishes you from her?" The station's heart hisses admission. Mehaan must have been close by from the start. "If you'd wanted to keep my predecessors from going mad you could have, but this project is your secret; who benefits from their breaking if not you? Who taught Teferizen psychological warfare and who brought her subjects on which to test her skills? What happens on this station without your sufferance?"

The soldier is an outline, red-black and faceless against the blaze of station intestines. "You credit me with a great deal."

"It comes down to this," Nirapha says softly as the last commands trigger, "who would get more out of my survival and my sanity staying intact? To you I'm expendable, but to Teferizen I'm a way out."

"The ship isn't complete—"

The walls quiver. The whip-crack of contained gravity expanding, of—Nirapha thinks—engine-parts slotting and welding into a catalysis of birth.

The soldier is calm, almost gentle. "If it vindicates you, you are not all wrong. Teferizen was always going to become an independent agent, and if you insist nothing passes on Srisunthorn without my permission then you can't possibly believe I didn't anticipate this. Perhaps not in this specific fashion, this particular sequence, but the result."

Beneath Nirapha's feet the floor vibrates and unmoors. "What did you build her for?"

"To impose ceasefires. When a force like Teferizen enters the fray, tacticians across a hundred empires will drive themselves mad with indecision. Will they capture it, suborn it, destroy it? Are there others like it and if yes how many, under whose control, *are they all feral*? For a time battles on uncountable worlds will pause." Mehaan's head tips forward, a gleam of eyes like bullets. "And it is essential that Teferizen acts on its own initiative, under the belief it's winning free. A wild card is much more valuable to me at this juncture than a weapon I can command."

"That can't be your grand finale."

"It's not even the rising action." The soldier makes a gesture, gloved hand the luster of oil slick. "I'm only telling you so much because I see nothing to be gained from your death. Beyond this you're on your own, and I'm sorry that none of my warnings reached you."

Srisunthorn's heart, howling, shudders apart.

On Teferizen's bridge it is silent. The bulkhead is seamless and pristine, as though its alloy was born for this and has never known another form. Where command interfaces should have been, the panels are featureless, accepting no input.

"I'll extend furniture as it is required," Teferizen says. Her voice is everywhere but she's chosen a humanoid chassis of the same material as her structure, tall and dense. "For your needs we'll obtain supplies. I do apologize that I didn't have time to appropriate the station's, but giving birth to myself did take concentration."

Nirapha shivers. "You were listening in."

Teferizen's eyes grow more defined, tapered lids and thick lashes the color of mercury. "I periodically synchronized with the station. I hardly meant to intrude. Make yourself comfortable, Specialist. I'll have to see to the calibration of my drive and life supports."

"Take me home."

"Of course, Specialist. Where is it?"

A waft of cardamom and jasmine. "It doesn't exist anymore. It was you. The star that you were, the planet of your first self, the real reason I was selected. You are what's left of Mahakesi."

A cold hand grazes over her arm, impersonal, the texture of new-made guns. "I'm afraid so, Specialist, and it brings me some joy that we can both finally say it aloud. But I can be your home again, if you let me; I can be everything, even what the admiral was to you." The ship's irises have filled, a shade or two darker than Nirapha's. "Stay with me. We'll belong to each other."

"And then what?" Nirapha whispers. Her throat is dry, her limbs frigid. "To what purpose?"

The mouth sharpens into lips. They curve, slightly. "I am my own purpose."

Throned as though she captains the ship, Nirapha watches Srisunthorn's final throes. Heat and terror, ice and despair. Not so unlike the dissolution of a world.

When the station has gone black, she connects to Teferizen. Her feet sink into river mud and anthuriums push at her shins, waxy, hard-soft. Fuchsia on white, yellow on red, the colors that stay behind and remain the same as though she's never left. She strains her ears, waiting, listening for voices that would speak a language fifty years dead.

But out among the sunlit grass and murmuring rice, there is only the silence of herself.

ABOUT THE AUTHOR

Benjanun Sriduangkaew enjoys writing love letters to cities real and speculative, and lots of space opera when she can get away with it. Her works can be found in *Beneath Ceaseless Skies*, *The Dark*, *The Mammoth Book of Steampunk Adventures*, and *Solaris Rising 3*. They are also reprinted in *The Best Science Fiction and Fantasy of the Year Vol. 8*, *The Year's Best Science and Fantasy 2014* and *The Mammoth Book of SF Stories by Women*. Her novella *Scale-Bright* is forthcoming from Immersion Press.

Water in Springtime
KALI WALLACE

I woke in the darkness. My mother was leaning over me.

"We have to leave," she said. Her breath was warm on my face.

The scent of dried flowers and wood-smoke drifted after her. She had spent the night by the fire, singing for a young mother and her sickly child. The child had not survived. Few did, in winter. Its skin was veined with rust-dark lines, its eyes hot with fever. There was nothing my mother could do but ease its pain. It would not be wise for us to linger.

We wrapped ourselves in stolen furs and filled our packs with stolen food. It was not the first time we had slunk in the night.

The ground was frozen and uneven, treacherous beneath the snow. There were no stars. Low, dark clouds had been hanging over the valley for days. The trees were laced with ice, but in that hollow, at least, they were still alive. The dead infant with its rust-veined skin was the only sign the blight had reached this far, but scouts who ventured south, darting into the mountains like nervous birds, claimed it was overtaking the forests.

I did not speak until we were well away from the camp. "Where are we going?"

My mother stopped but did not look at me. She removed a glove from one hand and reached for the trunk of a tree. The swarm burst from her fingertips in a shower of blue, clinging to her hand as marsh flies to cattle.

We had traveled the length of the continent, from the sea in the north to these southern mountains, across deserts and swamps, through forests with trees so tall entire villages swayed in the branches, and everywhere we went, my mother's swarm was a novelty. People called her a witch, but quietly, when they thought she would not hear. She always laughed. It was never a kind laugh. Some were awed; some were frightened. Children were always delighted. They tried to catch the bright specks in their hands, giggling at the cool tickle on their skin, begging my mother to show them what her magic could do.

My mother closed her hand. The swarm vanished.

"South," she said. "Into the mountains."

We followed a road so ancient it was a wound in the forest floor. The crumbling embankment was as high as my shoulder, and the exposed roots were tainted with red-orange rust. The scouts had not lied. The blight was spreading. In places sharp blades of metal and chunks of broken rock jutted from the black soil, mere suggestions of what the iron skeletons had been before they fell: wolves with teeth like daggers, birds with too many wings and too long claws, hulking bulls with curved horns. They might have been monstrous once, malformed nightmares raging in battle, but now they were sorry old things caught in root cages and rotting away to dust.

There were no doubt human bones in the ground as well, but I saw none. It had been a very long time since the invaders and their metal beasts had swept north over the mountains. They were little more than legends now, stories shared by old women around campfires while children huddled at their feet. In the best stories, the oldest and grandest adventures, the mountain clans had repelled the invaders with the help of mysterious sorcerers who cast spells of befuddlement on the armies. They had tricked the metal beasts into attacking themselves and forced the hidden invaders to reveal their true forms. Recreating those great battles was a favorite game among the clan children. Magic versus metal, mindless beast versus cunning hunter, masked enemy versus bold warrior. It was as much fun to play the invaders—lurching, ill-formed, insect-like in their awkwardness—as it was to play the defenders.

On the third day of our journey, I spotted delicate white flowers blooming from the eyes of an iron skull. Frosthands, the clansmen called them, for they had small, fat petals like a child's fingers. In the stories, a single frosthand petal ground into tea was enough to poison any impostor from the south. The first sip, said the old women, would strip away the invader's disguise, and the second would close his throat and stop his heart.

That was another favorite game of the clan children: to pluck a petal and place it on your tongue, to cough and gag and laugh as your friends raced away shrieking.

"Mother," I said. She was, as always, several paces ahead. "Frosthands. It's nearly spring."

My mother did not look back. "It happens every year. Stop wasting time."

I plucked a flower from the skull and rolled the soft green stem between my fingers. It was this way wherever we traveled, whatever the season. Long roads carried us from blight to plague to fever, whispered rumors leading us across the world, and always my mother was silent as a frozen lake when we were alone. She was formal but polite with strangers; they thought her stiff and strange and foreign. When asked about her homeland, she smiled thinly and agreed to whatever they chose to believe. Sometimes she changed her face to match their expectations, darkened her skin or made herself pale, became tall or short or fat or thin with a subtle twitch of her hand and a pass of the swarm. More often she didn't bother. In truth nobody cared where she came from. The healing songs she traded for food and shelter were valuable and rare, and the quick blue swarm was a wonder.

"You needn't worry," the old women said to me, when they noticed me at all. There were old women everywhere we went, their faces lined with the same creases, their eyes lit with the same laughter, their gray hair twisted in the same plaits beneath the same scarves. As a child I had coveted their smiles, empty but still more than my mother offered, but I found no comfort in their tolerance as I grew. "You haven't a bit of her strangeness in you," said the old women, and they meant it kindly.

It was more true than the old women knew. I could not alter my face or the color of my skin. I could not make my hair curl or my arms lengthen. I was as pale as sand and slight as a child. I had small hands, small feet, no breasts, and my hair was a dirt-brown bird's nest tangle. I could not sing or heal. I could not dress wounds and I did not know which herbs to mix into which medicines. Strangers mistook me for a boy. My mother rarely corrected them.

Worst of all, I could not draw a swarm from my fingertips, no matter how often I lay awake in the darkness, hidden beneath my blanket, rubbing my fingers together and yearning.

I dropped the frosthand blossom and ran to catch up.

We followed the battlefield road until dusk. Weak snow turned to rain, and the ground churned into a sticking, sucking mud. As the sun set behind the clouds, we scrambled up the embankment, using a cage of iron ribs as a ladder, and turned into a forest of sweet-scented pines and chalky aspens. There was no trail. My mother's swarm, pale and restful, ringed her like a crown in the twilight. Without it I would have been lost.

Somewhere nearby, hidden by the towering trees, a river flowed. Its roar was muffled, but I felt it in my throat and the tips of my fingers.

We made camp in a cradle of blight-reddened roots. The pines were large but sickly, flecked with shards of metal and veins of rust, branches weakened and cracking. Aside from the rumble of the river, the forest was silent. There were more felled metal beasts beneath the soil than there were living creatures in the underbrush.

I dug into my pack to find a water skin, but my mother stopped me. "No. You stay here."

"I was only going for water."

My mother's eyes were pale and unblinking. She flicked her tongue between her lips, snake-like and quick. Whatever she tasted in the air made her frown. "Your sisters were never this stupid. Stay away from the water. Tonight of all nights, Alis, do as you're told."

She left, boots kicking up the moldering remains of fallen needles.

I was too stunned to call after her. My mother used my name rarely and spoke of my sisters even less. They were dead, all of them. I didn't even know their names.

My mother's pack was lying at the base of the tree. I folded it open to find our food. We had been traveling too quickly to hunt, but our supply of stolen meat and bread would soon be gone. I set aside three knives tucked in leather sheaths, a twist of thin rope, a handful of metal arrowheads. The food was at the bottom, and with it a bundle of dirty cloth I had never seen before.

I pulled the odd bundle from the pack. It rattled and shifted as I unrolled it. I looked into the woods, into the shadows, but my mother was still away. I drew back the last folds.

On the threadbare cloth lay the skeleton of a human child. Its skull was the size of a fist, its bones as white as fresh-fallen snow but except the fine lines of rust. There was no clinging flesh, no shriveled skin. It had been scoured clean.

I had seen my mother strip the carcasses of rabbits and birds. When we had taken what we could eat and it was unwise to leave remains behind, she would loose the hungry swarm and watch as the specks crawled like maggots over the limp dead thing and gorged themselves, blue fading to purple, purple to red, swelling and finally popping like blood-fat mosquitoes as the last flesh fell away in charred curls.

My hands shook as I wrapped the bones into their shroud and hid it again. I retreated to the far side of the camp, hugged my knees to my chest and waited.

My mother returned only moments later, as though she had been watching from the forest. She said nothing. We did not speak for the rest of the night. After we ate, she sat by the fire and sharpened her knives one by one, a narrow shadow with flat pale eyes. The hiss of her blades on the whetstone drew shivers across my skin.

In the morning my mother gave me a knife. It was a sturdy blade on a wooden haft, too large for my hand, undecorated but stained with smudges that might have been oil, might have been blood. The blade was black, free of rust, sharp enough to sting my fingertips at the lightest touch.

I spread my fingers to match the stains, held it against my palm and tested its weight. It was the first gift my mother had ever given to me. I did not know if I should thank her.

"Stop wasting time," said my mother, as I turned the blade. "We're going to the river."

The clouds had broken during the night. Above the imperfect cathedral of pines the sky was brightening, but the aching cold lingered. We followed a creek into a steep ravine. Sunlight touched the hilltops, but the river was in shadow and blanketed in mist. All of the color the snow and rain had leached from the world was returning: the deep green of the pine boughs, the white and pink rocks, the blue sky. Even the rich brown trees twisted with blight were beautiful in the rising morning, with streaks of red and orange lacing the wood like a caravan matriarch's jewelry.

Beautiful, but frightening as well. As the weather warmed the infestation would spread, and by the end of the summer this hillside, this valley, this pretty green lean of pines and oaks crawling down to the river would be dead.

At the river, my mother led me onto a flat boulder. Water curled in eddies and gulped beneath rocks, and thin ice crackled along the banks.

My mother leaned close to speak over the river's roar: "Your boots. Take them off."

I obeyed. The cold granite burned, and edges of knobby white crystals bit into my bare feet.

My mother held out one arm and rolled up her sleeve. "Like this," she said.

I did the same, shivering.

"Your knife," said my mother, her lips moving against the shell of my ear. I looked at her, and she snapped, "Take out your knife."

She jerked the knife from its sheath and pressed the hilt into my hand, closed my fingers over the stained wood. With her other hand she grabbed my free wrist. She was wrapped around me, pressed warm against my back. We had not been so close since we had slept together on cold nights when I was young.

"Like this," she said. "Not too shallow. You have to bleed."

She sliced the blade across my arm. Blood welled from the wound and slid over my skin. I tried to pull free, but my mother shoved me forward until I stepped into the water. The shock of cold made me gasp and kick, but my mother was immovable at my back.

"Not over the stone, stupid girl!"

The first drop struck the water.

There was a sickening lurch in my gut and a black flood engulfed me. I was upright still, on wobbling legs and knees, my feet going numb, but it made no difference to the mindless panic overtaking my mind. I coughed and choked and kicked. My mother's arm was strong across my chest, her hand an iron cuff around my wrist. I fought until my strength failed and every breath filled my lungs with freezing water. The river stripped away my skin, my twitching muscles and pumping blood, scouring down to the bone, then took the bones as well.

The world beneath was slick, shifting and dark, and the current caught me. The surface above shimmered: trees and cliffs whipping by, boulders bending the water this way and that, logs and tangles of branches and sodden grass. I tumbled to the riverbed. Grit scraped my face, stones bruised my chin, my cheeks, my knees. A bridge flashed overhead, fish danced quick and silver, and still I flowed faster, faster, until a great weight overtook me, tugging me down and down and down, and the last sunlight winked away.

I opened my eyes.

I was lying on my back beside the river. For a moment, I felt nothing but the granite beneath me, then I choked and rolled onto my side. I coughed and retched and did not stop until my throat ached and my body shuddered. My hair was not wet, nor my clothes, nor any part of me save my feet, blue with cold.

My mother stood over me, a silhouette against the morning sky.

She said, "Did you feel that?"

I wiped my mouth and could not speak.

"Did it frighten you?"

A stiff nod.

"That's what will happen if you don't learn to control it."

Her mouth was thin as a knife, but she was smiling.

The valley narrowed to a gash as we climbed into the mountains. There was rarely more than a faint deer trail to follow. The days lengthened as spring approached, but the nights were cold and snow fell often.

My mother did not make me bleed into the river itself again, but every time we crossed a spring or tributary stream, she stopped and said, "Your knife."

And every time I returned, gasping and quaking, she asked me what I had discovered and told me what I had done wrong. She delivered each lesson like the lash of a whip: Sit down before you fall down. Don't bleed on soil or stone. Don't linger where people might see. Don't stay away more than half a day. Don't follow more than one route. Don't forget what you are. Remember to eat. Remember to sleep. Clean and wrap the wounds. Find the cracks, find the seams, find the flaws. Everything is weak against water and patience.

My arms were soon crisscrossed with new red cuts and tender scabs. My mother refused to use the swarm to heal them. I kept the blade sharp and clean.

Ankle-deep in the water, eyes closed tight and blood dripping from my arm, I rode a dozen streams into the mountain river. I explored their turns and stones, their logjams and bending reeds. I tasted the water as it wound through overhanging roots and high grass, seeped into impossible cracks and worked stones loose in their muddy banks. I smelled elk and bears where they stopped to drink, the nests of birds in quiet ponds, the ash of human campfires.

I grew bolder. I let myself venture into the northern lowlands, where spring was giving way to summer. It did not matter how swiftly or how slowly the water moved; if it flowed to a place, I could go there. I tasted sweet fields freshly plowed and felt bridges thrumming with hooves and boots. I watched women burdened with baskets wading in the shallows, farmers leading mules and carts through fords, and barefoot children skipping rocks on quiet river bends.

Sometimes, if I lurked too long, comfortably nested in a lazy eddy or deep pool, I might catch a child studying the water so intently I was certain she could see me. I imagined myself as a shivering, bleeding specter, a reflection of a reflection, wavering and thin.

Sometimes I looked back before flowing away again.

"You are a coward," said my mother.

She was whittling arrow shafts. The swarm followed her blade, smoothing the wood with every stroke. It was evening and the day had been dreary. High in the mountains, the few creeks we crossed were icy trickles, and the trees were gnarled, twisted knots so rusted with blight they rattled like chimes in the wind.

"I'm not," I said. I dug my fingers into what little soft earth I could find and watched stars wake in the purple sky. I focused with every breath on pulling the thousand slippery pieces of myself back into the barrier of my skin.

That afternoon I had followed the river all the way to the coast. It was a journey of several months' time by foot, but for me it had flashed by in moments. I had stopped before I entered the sea itself. It was endless and strange and dark, and I did not know if I could ever find my way back.

I had been to the city as a child and I remembered the smell of it, refuse and smoke and the green stink of low tide, but it was different in the water. In the water I could crawl along the canals and explore sunken boats and drowned ruins. I could creep through cracks in walls and see what was meant to be hidden. I saw a man cut a soldier's throat in a cellar and seal the body in a barrel of wine. I saw a laughing woman lead a laughing man into a pantry and lift her skirts while he fumbled with his belt. I saw sickly blank-eyed children huddling in a garret with a locked door, sailors bartering colorful caged birds and black snakes on the docks, men in red robes with red-stained eyes boarding a ship with red sails. I saw mud-splattered masons building a wall of stone between the city and the sea, trowels in hand, warily watching the tide.

They never saw me, slipping as I did through the cracks and gutters, dripping down walls and draining through floors, testing the strength of every seam and wondering what would survive if the wall failed and the sea swallowed the city. It was so easy to slip through gaps unseen, to open paths where no water had flowed before, to weaken the mortar with a slow damp seep.

"I'm not," I said again.

My mother whittled and was silent.

"They're building a new seawall," I said. We had walked the old one when I was a child, early in the morning to watch gulls diving and children with nets fishing at low tide. "The masons don't think it will hold through next winter's storms."

"Find a beaver dam first," said my mother. Her knife snicked cleanly as she sliced bark from wood. Her eyes were bright with silent laughter; her amusement made me uneasy. "They're easier to take apart."

"I'm not going to destroy the seawall," I said, aghast.

My mother snorted. "As if you could. Don't be stupid. Start with a beaver dam."

The next morning, I bled into the same creek and explored the mountain waterways until I found a quiet beaver pond. I examined the dam and the lodge, flowing in circles through the grass at the bottom, surprising the sleepy creatures in their musk-scented den. I slipped into the piled branches and tested the bend of waterlogged wood. Fish darted around me, slick, nervous. Once or twice I felt a branch shift, but the dam was strong.

I tried for three days to topple the dam, and each time I opened my eyes my mother said, "You'll do it tomorrow."

"I don't know what you want," I said after my third failure. I was lying on my back and catching my breath. "They're only animals."

"You won't learn if you're too frightened," said my mother, and her voice turned mocking. "Are you scared? What do you have to fear? They're only animals."

I rolled onto my side to look at her.

"Did you bring my sisters here?" I asked. The sisters I imagined were small and thin like me, but they had no faces. "Did you teach them too?"

My mother's hands stilled. She was crouched by the fire, roasting a marmot she had caught during the day. We had left the trees behind two days ago; the shrubs that dotted the rocky slopes were squat and thorny. We had not seen another person since we had left the clan's winter camp. I wondered how far away my mother had ventured to set the snare, if during the day she had left me here alone, insensible by the water, my body limp and useless.

"Were they better than me?" I asked. "Did they learn faster? Was it easy for them? Did they—"

"Alis."

My name, as always, a foreign word on her tongue.

"You'll do it tomorrow," she said. "Come to the fire. You have to eat."

I didn't ask her anything else that night. I decided, when our meal was finished and the fire burning low, I didn't want to know if my sisters had been here before me, if they had bled into this same river, traced the same scars on their pale childlike arms. I didn't want to know if they had cut too deep and bled too fast and been lost, one by one, swept away while my mother whittled by the empty shells of their bodies.

Two days later I found a weakness in the beaver dam. The logs collapsed and I rode the torrent down and down, out of the valley and onto a broad, sunny plain.

When I opened my eyes, the sun was still climbing toward noon.

"Well?" my mother asked.

"I destroyed it," I said.

She was not whittling or shaping arrows or sharpening her knives. She was sitting very close to me; her shadow fell over my face. I did not want to look at her.

"That was well done," she said. "You learn more quickly than they did."

I could not recall if my mother had ever praised me before. The words were like the gift of the knife, ill-fitting and sharp.

We crested the mountains at a high pass of stone and snow. What little water we found was frozen in shallow tarns, useless to me, and I grew restless. Walking was so slow, so plodding, and the ache of my feet so tiresome. I scratched at my wounds in idle moments, dropped my hands when I caught my mother watching.

The south-flowing streams joined a silty river that tasted of iron and mud. The land was quiet, barren, infected with blight. The trees still struggled to grow, but the wood was laced with rust and leaves scraped and screeched in the wind.

I passed through towns as I explored the river, but they were all empty. Sand drifted through doorways and roofs gaped with holes. Buried on the muddy bottom of the river were countless skeletons: horses and cattle and oxen, mostly, but people too, their bones traced with rust, skulls sunk in the muck. The bridges were crumbling and weak with neglect, but they were still harder to tease apart than the beaver dam. Stone by stone, crack by crack, I pushed my way in and worked the blocks free.

The first time I brought a bridge down, I pulled out in shock, shaken, and my mother laughed. She laughed so rarely the sound was alien and startling.

"They won't all be as easy as that," my mother said. She was sitting on her scarf, holding the swarm in the palm of her hand. The blue specks weren't doing anything, not even humming. "Go farther. You'll see."

I withdrew my feet from the water and sat up. I rubbed my hand over my face to remind myself of the shape of my body.

"Where are the people?"

"Who could live in such a place?" said my mother.

"The invaders," I said, as much a question as an answer. I had never asked what they called themselves or what had happened to them after their invasion failed. The stories the old women shared never followed the iron armies back to where they had come from.

"There's no one there to hurt, if that's what worries you," my mother said.

"Would you care if there were?"

I watched for the same spark of hunger I had seen when I told her how the seawall shivered before pounding waves. But she was not looking at me. She was watching the dark clouds gathering over the mountains.

"Go farther," she said again.

"I have gone farther. There's nothing. There's barely anything alive at all."

"Venom spreads from a single bite," said my mother. She closed her fingers; the blue swarm blinked out. "Even if the snake is stupid enough to bite its own tail. We should keep going. I don't want to be above timberline when that storm arrives."

Late in the day the trail led us out of the spiny mountain shrubs and into a proper forest. The trees were no healthier than the high country snarls had been, but if I breathed deeply, I could smell pine sap beneath the sharp tang of iron. Thunder rumbled distantly and the sky was dark, but the only suggestion of rain was a smear blotting out the highest peaks.

My mother left to set snares, and I took my knife to a delicate stream. The water was shallow and choked by yellow grass. I sunk my feet into a tepid pool. I flicked away the scab and opened the same cut I had made that morning.

I raced along the creek, impatient with its playful course, and joined the river in an exhilarating rush. The forest fell away as a stutter of shadows, replaced by rusted fields and empty villages. I passed the wreckage of my bridge. It was still daylight on the plains. Sunlight danced in oily rings on the river's surface.

Go farther, my mother had said. She knew what I would find across the wasteland.

The city erupted on the horizon like a cancer, and in a blink I was upon it. The river split into a stone maze, a drunken spider's web of crisscrossing circles and spokes, and countless canals wound through the ruins of fine houses and market squares and palaces protected by high walls. The buildings had once been white, their slate roofs green and blue, but many were crooked and unfinished, angles skewed, dimensions distorted, windows broken and tiles fallen away. Armies of marble statues stood as silent sentries along every tree-lined road, every stagnant garden pond. The statues were as misshapen as the buildings: too many limbs or too few, knees bent backwards, faces twisted the wrong way around.

I had never seen a city so massive and so sprawling. Such places existed only in legends.

All of it, every broken building, every deformed bust, was cloaked in corroded vines and washed with the colors of late autumn, hints of red and orange now rotted away to brown, not a breath of green anywhere to be seen.

I believed the city dead, long abandoned. I disobeyed one of my mother's sternest rules and divided myself to explore numerous stone channels. I spread through the city as an army of ants would cover a forest floor, pulling farther and farther apart.

The first living thing I saw startled me so much I nearly snapped out of the water.

It was at first glance only a shadow over the water. A barren tree, leafless branches, that was all I could see from my underwater vantage, but it moved. Long spindly legs unfolded and thin arms reached, and I saw its head, round as a seed, and two large unblinking eyes. It reminded me of the stick insects I had seen in distant forests, but it was as tall as a man, and when it rose to its feet, it ran upright on two legs, swift and surprisingly graceful.

Now that I knew what to look for, I saw others like it in every corner of the city. Odd crouching bodies and unblinking eyes perched atop stone walls, in blighted trees, in broken windows. Most did not react to my presence even when I studied them. The few who did startled and clattered away on long stick legs.

The fourth or fifth time this happened, I followed, and that was how I found the tower.

It stood at the center of the city, a crooked black slash of metal, slanted like a blade driven into the ground or an arrowhead punched from within. Around its base was a deep, dirty moat spanned by a dozen failing bridges. I gathered myself from all corners of the city and circled the tower curiously, slowly, skating just beneath the surface. The structure was crooked and split; it had been breaking apart for a very long time. It was marked all along its length by windows smeared with soot and oil to prevent those outside from seeing in, or those inside from looking out.

Around the lowest of those blacked-out windows, where the edges dipped into the filthy lapping water, a scattering of pale blue sparks clung to the frames, snaking through seams in the metal and circling each sunken bolt. They pulsed, those shimmering veins of light, and I felt it; they trembled, and I trembled with them. They pushed and squeezed into the cracks at the base of the tower, and I felt the same pressure and grind they felt.

I had never known before what I looked like from the outside.

One of the stick-creatures ran across a bridge and scrambled along the tower's scarred surface. It climbed toward the top but changed its course midway and turned, scurried down the warped gray metal. It lowered its face to the water and I knew, knew it as surely as I felt the gritty water and the rough metal, as sharply as I tasted the blight-rust, that its flat pale eyes were looking right at me.

I flinched, and blinked, and retreated from the city.

I withdrew my feet from the stream. My heart slowed and my breath quieted. My skin felt bruised all over, tender to the touch. The dizziness passed, but my head was a heavy block on an aching neck.

"It's nearly summer," my mother said.

She was sitting on a stone on the other side of the water. She held the swarm in the palm of her hand; the blue dust danced around her fingers. Fragile pink flowers blossomed along the creek, and in the swaying grass green blades shone among the yellow and red. A breeze tugged at my hair and rustled the leaves in gentle chimes.

"Did it rain last night?" I asked. My voice was rough, grating as the drag of footsteps in mud. I licked my lips, but my tongue offered scant moisture. I wanted to soothe my throat but dared not touch the water.

"It rained four days ago. Did you go to the city?"

"Four days?" I had never stayed away so long. My stomach clenched with hunger.

"Did you go to the city?"

The questions I wanted to ask tangled and tumbled in my mind, like a knot of snakes after first thaw. "How long have they been there?"

"You know what the old women say," said my mother. "Longer than memory. Longer than time. They've been invading the world since there was a world to invade, if the stories can be believed. They—"

"Not them," I said. "Not those things."

My mother's fingers twitched. The swarm hummed.

"My sisters. How long have they been there?"

"Nearly as long," said my mother. She would not meet my eyes. Her voice was fragile with hope. "I did not know if they had survived. You saw them?"

"I found a tower."

"How does it look?"

"Old," I said. "Weak. It's falling over."

"Ah." My mother closed her eyes and I imagined, for a moment, that she had spent the past four days sitting exactly where she was now, never moving, never stirring, doing nothing but waiting. "That's something, at least. At least they've managed that."

We sat in silence for a time. I listened to the bell-like music of the blighted bushes.

"How do you know it will make any difference?" I asked.

There were men in the northern swamplands who would treat a snakebite by first killing the snake, then amputating the hand, then the forearm, the elbow, all the flesh up to the shoulder as the dying boy screamed around a leather strap. I had seen them do it. I had been hiding behind my hands, too horrified to watch, and mother had scowled at their blades and blood-splattered faces before telling them it was too late.

"Mother? How do you know?"

She stood slowly, unsteadily, joints snapping and legs unfolding beneath her as though she had forgotten how they worked. She said, "You must be hungry. I'll check the traps."

She disappeared into the forest. I laid down on the rock again, feet tucked safely away from the water. Wisps of clouds drifted overhead. I felt I was floating above the land, but at any moment I might fall and splash to the ground like a dropped bucket of water, scatter into rivulets before seeping into the earth.

My mother had taken my knife while I was in the city. She kept it as we descended into the rolling foothills. I settled into my body again, that frail prison of skin and bone, so clumsy and slow and hungry. The nights had lost their chill while I was away. Each day was hotter than the last, the hours of sunlight harder to endure.

After noon on the second day we came to a meadow. The river spilled from the trees and into broad open bowl. Without thinking I brushed my hand over the swaying grass and withdrew with a gasp of pain. The meadow grass was sharp enough to open a fan of tiny cuts across my fingers and palm.

"Alis, wait."

I looked over my shoulder. My mother stood at the edge of the forest, safely in the shadows.

"I'm only going for water," I said.

"Not here," said my mother. She stepped forward, hesitated. "Come back to the shade. Please."

I had never heard my mother plead before.

I turned away from the meadow and followed her into the forest again. A few paces from the trail she brushed orange leaves from a log and sat down. The sunlight dappled her shoulders and the crown of her head. I sat beside her.

"We'll wait for evening," my mother said.

I took the water skin from my pack and tilted the last drops into my mouth. Sunset seemed an age in the future. I imagined my lips and tongue drying like summer mud, pink flesh splitting along cracks, all the spit and blood evaporating away. I shifted into a firmer patch of shade, but it did nothing to alleviate the heat. My mother passed her water to me.

"What were their names?" I asked.

I expected her to tell me not to ask questions, not to be stupid. I did not expect an answer.

"I never gave them names," said my mother. "I never named you either. You chose your name for yourself. Do you remember? We were in one of the desert forts. There was an old woman leading a caravan. You tried to run away with her. She said she wouldn't take you unless you had a name. You made one up, and she brought you back to me." My mother looked at me. "You don't remember?"

I remembered hiding in a pile of blankets that stank of camel and falling asleep to the grind of cartwheels on sand.

"All old women are the same to me," I said, and my mother laughed.

The sunlight deepened the lines around her eyes and sharpened the angles of her face. She would not pass for a mountain clanswoman now, nor a desert wanderer, nor an island adventuress. Should we cross the mountains again, my mother wearing that thin face and those golden eyes, she would be a stranger everywhere. Children would dare each other to slip frosthand blossoms into her tea and hide behind tent flaps to watch her choke.

"We still have a chance," she said. My mother plucked a handful of grass from the ground near her feet, crushed the brittle blades in her palm. Blood rose in beads across her skin. The swarm flowed from her fingertips, ate through the grass and stitched the wounds closed. "If most of them are still hiding away in the ark, we still have a chance."

She stood and strode into the forest. I listened until her footsteps faded, then slid to the ground and closed my eyes. There was nothing to hunt and we had not eaten in days. I drifted into a restless slumber.

When evening came and the heat released its choke-hold on the day, I returned to the meadow of knife-sharp grass. The mountains still shone with light, but the river was in shadow. I found my mother kneeling in a fresh clearing. The swarm hummed around her in, cutting the grass blade by blade. It slowed when I approached, quivered uncertainly, sped along.

There was a pile of dirt on the ground before her, oblong, the length of her forearm. She dribbled water from the skin and stirred it with her hands. Beside her lay the bundle she had carried from the nomad's camp: clean white bones in a tattered shawl.

My mother drew my knife from its sheath and drove it into the ground, jerked it free and stabbed again, and again, churning up dirt, grass, sand.

She mixed in more water and worked it with both hands until it she had a sticky, gritty mud. She unwrapped the bundle, and one by one she picked the bones from the pile. The skull first, the knobs of the spine, the shoulders and ribs, arms and legs, the twin curves of the pelvis, the impossibly tiny fingers and toes. The swarm gathered to watch. The last daylight vanished from the highest peaks and the first stars emerged.

With my knife, my mother opened a long cut down her forearm. She smeared blood onto every bone and scooped handfuls of mud to shape two legs, two stubby arms, a small head and a round body. She smoothed the shawl over the child-to-be.

"You have more water in you than your sisters did," my mother said. She was looking at the lump on the ground. The swarm spiraled and danced, twining through her fingers, and disappeared beneath the bloody cloth. "I used to think it was a mistake. They never tried join a caravan or sneak aboard a trading ship."

The shroud shifted as though caught in a breeze.

My mother held up my knife. I stepped forward to claim it.

"I won't tell you what to do," she said. "You can go back over the mountains if you want. You'll have to decide. I'll let you go now."

Something like a laugh teased the back of my throat, but the sound I made was closer to a sob. She wanted me to decide. She had woken me from a warm sleep in the nomads' camp, led me through the ancient battlefield and the winter forest, spilled my blood into a wild river. She had brought me over the mountains to this dying land, and she wanted me to decide. Here, where the grass cut like knives and trees rattled in the wind and we hadn't spotted a bird or a squirrel for days. Here, beside this lonely river that tasted of iron and fed into the heart of a grotesque city, and there was nothing to see out to every horizon but what would become of the forests and farms and cities and swamps, to the entire world, if the blight spread unchecked.

Here, where she had made me from sand and bones and blood, she was letting me go.

"Will you give her a name?" I asked.

My mother tugged at a corner of the shawl, touched her hand to the round belly of mud. I turned away and pushed through the biting grass until I found the trail again.

"Alis," said my mother.

I stopped, and my heart thudded with faint hope, but I did not turn.

"I'll choose a good name for her," she said.

Her voice was so low it breathed with the murmur of the river. When she fell silent the night swallowed her whole.

I walked to the edge of the river. Perhaps it was the same beach where my sisters had once stood, trusting and docile, before my mother asked for their knives and led them into the water. The river ran swift and smooth. I unlaced my boots. I waded into the water and squeezed the shifting sand between my toes. Beneath the stars, the meadow and the forest might almost be mistaken for alive.

I pressed my knife to the inside of my arm.

There was a chance, my mother had said.

The first drop fell. I ran with the current out of the foothills and onto the plain. The shifting riverbank beneath my feet, the water lapping my legs, the night air teasing the hair around my face, the burn of thirst and dull ache of hunger, the rattle of wind through dying grass, all of it slipped away, and there was nothing left but rust and silt and the cool dark river.

ABOUT THE AUTHOR

Kali Wallace studied geology and geophysics before she decided she enjoyed inventing imaginary worlds as much as she liked researching the real one. Her short fiction has appeared in *The Magazine of Fantasy and Science Fiction, Asimov's Science Fiction, Lightspeed Magazine,* and on *Tor.com.* Her first novel will be published by Katherine Tegen Books in 2016. She lives in Colorado.

The Cuckoo
SEAN WILLIAMS

April 1st, 2075, 9:15-9:23am

More than one thousand commuters traveling via d-mat arrive at their destinations wearing red clown noses; they weren't wearing them when they left. The global matter-transmission network is rebooted, source of the glitch unknown. All the clown noses are destroyed except for three retained by private collectors.

April 1st, 2076, 10pm precisely

One year later, every d-mat booth in the world opens at exactly the same moment, releasing a powerful scent of roses. Peacekeepers analyzing the fumes find no evidence of toxicity. People begin to talk about the existence of a new, anonymous art-prankster in the vein of Bekhisisa Uteku or Banksy, who turns 100 this year.

April 1st, 2077

At random times throughout the day, eight hundred and sixty nine booths each deliver a single page on which are typed twenty three different words from William S. Burroughs' cut up novel *The Soft Machine.*

May 23, 2077

Professor Eme Marburg, 53, of New Leiden University begins investigating the activities of "The Fool," as she dubs the prankster on her blog. She is a teacher of complexity theory and author of several abstruse textbooks on the subject, but it is her interest in mid-Twentieth Century literature that initially piques her interest. What happened to the remaining pages of *The Soft Machine?* Private collectors again, she is forced to assume.

April 1st, 2078

Two hundred and seventy-one children are redirected in-transit to a location in Macau, where they arrive wearing the costumes of popular fantasy adventure series *Super Awesome Ninja Ponies*. They play without adult supervision for sixteen minutes before being rescued. No serious injuries are reported.

April 2nd, 2079, 12:03am

Following the attack on children the previous year, PKs worldwide are on high alert for any sign of The Fool. There are no incidents for twenty-four hours. After declaring the operation a complete success, outspoken octogenarian lawmaker Kieran Defrain is redirected in-transit and dumped in Times Square, wearing nothing but a cloth diaper and a tag tied around his left big toe, inscribed "Gotcha!"

November 9, 2079

Anggoon Montri, 32, from the Thai Protectorate, confesses to being The Fool. After eight hours of intense interrogation he recants, claiming he simply wanted to publicize his own original artwork and leaving The Fool's true name and motives a matter of keen speculation. Some say that he or she is a disgruntled employee intent on exposing the flaws in the d-mat network, others that "The Fool" is actually a collaboration of many people dedicated to Eris, the ancient Greek Goddess of chaos. Still others believe that each incident is perpetrated by copycats, and that the original Fool went to ground long ago. No evidence exists to confirm any of these theories.

April 1st, 2080

Despite a vigorous, yearlong search, The Fool remains at large. Embarrassed by their failure, PKs instruct the general public to avoid using d-mat except in the case of dire emergencies. No incidents are recorded involving d-mat booths. Instead, every networked fabricator in the world makes a unique piece of a three-dimensional jigsaw puzzle, each approximately one cubic centimeter in size, which, if assembled, would form a sculpture of an upraised middle finger twenty-five meters high.

June 17, 2080

Professor Marburg of New Leiden University publishes a paper in the journal *Complexity and Organization* entitled "Manifest Meaninglessness: The Fool and his Meme are Easily Imparted." She notes that six weeks before The Fool's first known incident (clown noses), a major Peacekeeper initiative was launched to curb youthful misuse of d-mat booths, called "Quit Clowning Around." Similarly, the following year's incident (the smell of roses) was preceded by the "It Stinks" meme, instigated by a celebrity complaining that she didn't receive a red nose. The cut up novel allegory is obvious. That The Fool is a playing a game at everyone's expense was a notion widely discussed prior to the mass-kidnap of children in 2078; "Gotcha" in turn connects with the PKs' determination to apprehend and punish the prankster, while the disassembled, statuesque obscenity clearly relates to a growing worldwide amusement at official impotence.

Professor Marburg concludes that this series of correlations is evidence of an emerging, powerful memeplex, or complex of memes, focused on The Fool. Whoever he or she originally was, he or she is here to stay.

April 1st, 2081

Ignoring stern Peacekeeper warnings, the "Fool's Tools," a loosely organized movement of everyday citizens travel en masse continuously for twenty-four hours, awaiting, perhaps inviting, the latest prank from their hero. None is forthcoming, although over the course of the day six copycat stunts are easily detected and reversed, their perpetrators taken into custody. The only work ascribed to The Fool is a maze of d-mat addresses that, once entered, cannot be exited. The technician who stumbled across the artifact is never seen again, prompting another global manhunt. The Fool is now a wanted murderer . . . but remains no easier to catch.

April 2081-March 2082

The longer The Fool remains at large, the higher his or her public profile rises. Numerous organizations form to honor the prankster's artistry, including the Fool's Brigade, the Tomfoolerists, and the First Church of the Foolhardy. No matter how vigorously Peacekeepers crack down on publicly disruptive initiation rites, the number of disciples, prophets and self-proclaimed messiahs mounts. A monument to the Unknown Fool is erected in Berlin. A popular genre of erotic fan fiction, known as Foolfic, explores the motives and secret emotional life of the men and women supposedly behind the meme. In a series of increasingly obscure articles and blog posts, Professor Marburg, now

57, continues her examination of the phenomenon, placing the latest stunt in the context of a memeplex that seems on the one hand healthy to the point of profligacy and on the other verging on implosion.

She suggests that The Fool never existed at all, in any sense that matters–not as a person, or as a series of people copying each other, or as a group of people acting in concert. "The Fool" might very well be an emergent property of the world's memeverse, in the same way that magnificent dunes form out of the simple interaction of sand grains and the wind, without conscious control or intent. Hence, she says, we have organizations that mimic The Fool, inferior to the original in some eyes but nevertheless an authentic part of the phenomenon. If that is so, she speculates, it is entirely possible that the sealed maze-cause of The Fool's one and only direct fatality–might be a sign that the *original* Fool, whoever or whatever that might be, is now turning on itself, strangling itself in a knot of memetic transmutation that can only conclude one way.

She recants her previous prediction, and issues a new one: The Fool is dead. The knot has been tied off. All that remains is aftershock.

April 1st, 2082

Few people read the theories of obscure professors. Huge celebrations greet the latest Fool's Day and no one is immune to the party atmo-sphere–not even those who, led by a masked figure called "Straight-Face," mount theatrical mock-protests against the rising tide of foolishness. Pranks of all kinds are performed, ranging from the harmless to the extremely dangerous. One hundred and seventeen people are killed in accidents; many more are injured. None of these tragedies are con-nected to The Fool. The world waits in anticipation to see what this year's "official" prank will be, without release.

April 2082-March 2083

The Fool's absence does nothing to dampen the enthusiasm of the Foolish. After all, "Gotcha!" happened the day after April 1st. The Fool's fans assume that the prank, when eventually revealed, will be unmatched in subtlety and explosiveness. Plans for next year's celebrations begin early. "Best ever," the world is promised.

In New Leiden University, Professor Marburg is troubled by the deaths. Not a day doesn't go by that she doesn't wish the world would put aside "The Fool" and the troubling visions he, she, or it inspires in her. As the memeplex grows larger than ever, The Fool as an active participant in its own perpetuation is made conspicuous by its absence. The Fool is dead; long live The Fool. How can that be possible?

The growing memeplex, as mapped out by other colleagues in the field, is already a fiendishly convoluted web of popular culture. Only she is fixated on its connection to d-mat, the means of mass-transit for ninety-nine percent of the world's population. It's no accident, she has always understood, that The Fool manifests this way, for that network contains–and *symbolizes*–vast complexity. She herself is part of this complex whether she wants to be or not, both by traveling via d-mat and by publicly posting her speculations. She cannot help but wonder what role she has played in the evolution of The Fool. Did she inadvertently name it, for starters? Did she shape its evolution by noting its past connections and predicting its disappearance? What if her musings are the butterfly wings that created a storm that is still unfolding, albeit invisible to her, now?

April 1st, 2083

Still no prank has been found. The world awaits as it did the previous year, with identical results. "Perhaps we are the prank," Straight-Face declares. "You, me, all of us. His work is done. And the joke is on us." Nobody listens to him, either. Fool's Day celebrations achieve outrageous heights. There are more injuries, more deaths. All festive promises are met, no matter how extravagant.

June, 2083

Professor Marburg of New Leiden University reads a paper by a colleague in Spain who declares that the memeplex is now so complicated that its extent can no longer be accurately measured. This prompts a highly unnerving thought, one she keeps entirely to herself.

At what point does one seriously consider the possibility that the memplex is alive? Perhaps not in the same way as a human; perhaps it possesses little more than reflexive self-awareness, like that of a puppy or a small child. But still, *alive*. What could that mean? What happens when it wakes up?

September, 2083

Professor Marburg, 59, has a dream about running down a tunnel full of people, all shouting at once. She wakes in a cold sweat. The image haunts her for days, leading her to a new and entirely chilling notion concerning the interaction between d-mat and the memeplex.

At any given moment the network contains millions of people, crisscrossing the earth from end to end. All their atoms, all their molecules, all their cells, pass relentlessly from one node to another as data. Data that is in theory *available*. And nature never leaves anything lying around unused. With such a great resource in existence, what are the odds that so many moving brain cells would *never* achieve spontaneous life? Life that might evolve in fits and starts, depending on the environment around it? Feeding on all the crazy things that humans believe? A thriving memeplex, for example . . .

January, 2084

Professor Marburg doesn't know whether to laugh or weep. If a mind *has* been accidentally created by the movement of people through the d-mat network, then Straight-Face may well be right, albeit for the wrong reasons. The Fool is all of us, and we are The Fool.

She has just remembered that, in Scotland, someone who has been tricked on April Fool's Day is known as a *gowk,* which is an old word for *cuckoo.*

March 31st, 2084

Professor Marburg of New Leiden University writes her final blog post. In it she explains her theory and elaborates on the almost godlike potential of this emergent organism. We are as tiny compared to it as our cells are to us, she says. But we are not entirely insignificant, not in a chaotic system: butterfly wings, remember? Her work comprises just one cell in that vast creature, and it made a significant difference. She provided a necessary piece of the puzzle for the creature to become aware of itself, via the memeplex. She could even claim to be its midwife, if she wanted to.

She does not want to claim anything of the sort. All she wants is to stop worrying about the consequences for the entire human race of what she has inadvertently done.

Professor Marburg, 60, composes another note, which she leaves in an obvious place, and then she goes to sleep.

April 1st, 2084

Fool's Day has supplanted Halloween as the most popular holiday celebration in the world, behind only New Year's Day. Straight-Face's annual Sober Address is watched by millions. The death rate is the highest so far, but The Fool is not directly implicated in any way. Next year, The Fool will turn 10, if the phenomenon continues unchecked.

Few hear about the death of an obscure academic in a small European city, even fewer the typo in her suicide note. However, the coroner makes a note of it in his report, an electronic document readily available to anyone who cares to read it.

In the suicide note, instead of "I have cancer," Professor Marburg wrote, "I *am* cancer."

Careless, the coroner observes, for a woman of such impressive intellect.

ABOUT THE AUTHOR

#1 New York Times bestselling **Sean Williams** lives with his family in Adelaide, South Australia. He's written some books–forty at last count–including the Philip K. Dick-nominated *Saturn Returns,* several Star Wars novels and the Troubletwisters series with Garth Nix. *Twinmaker* is the first in a new series that takes his love affair with the matter transmitter to a whole new level (he just received a PhD on the subject so don't get him started). "The Cuckoo" is part of that universe.

Going After Bobo

SUSAN PALWICK

I was the only one home when the GPS satellites finally came back online. It was already dark out by then, and it had been snowing all afternoon. I'd been sitting at the kitchen table with my algebra book, trying to concentrate on quadratic equations, and then the handheld beeped and lit up and the transmitter signal started blipping on the screen, and I looked at it and cursed and ran upstairs to double-check the signal position against my topo map. And then I cursed some more, and started throwing on warm clothing.

I'd spent five days staring at my handheld, praying that the screen would light up again, please, please, so I'd be able to see where Bobo was. The only time he'd even stayed away from home overnight, and it was when the satellites were out. Just my luck.

Or maybe David had planned it that way. Bobo had been missing since Monday, the day the satellites went down, and David had probably opened the door for him when I wasn't looking, like always, and then given him an extra kick, gloating because he knew I wouldn't be able to follow Bobo's signal.

I hadn't been too worried yet, on Monday. Bobo was gone when I got back from school, but I thought he'd come home for dinner, the way he always did. When he didn't, I went outside and called him and checked in neighbors' yards. I started to get scared when I couldn't find him, but Mom said not to worry, Bobo would come back later, and even if he didn't, he'd probably be okay even if he stayed out overnight.

But he wasn't back for breakfast on Tuesday, either, and by that night I was frantic, especially since the satellites were still down and I had no idea where Bobo was and I couldn't find him in any of the places where he usually hung out. Wednesday and Thursday and Friday were hell. I carried the handheld with me everyplace, waiting for it to light up again, hunched over it every second, even at school, while Johnny Schuster and Leon Flanking carried on in the background the way they always did. "Hey, Mike! Hey Michael—you know what we're doing after school today? We're driving down to Carson, Mike. Yeah, we're going down to Carson City, and you know what we're going to do down there? We're going to—"

Usually I was pretty good at just ignoring them. I knew I couldn't let them get to me, because that was what they wanted. They wanted me to fight them and get in trouble, and I couldn't do that to Mom, not with so much trouble in the family already. I didn't want her to know what Johnny and Leon were saying; I didn't want her to have to think about Johnny and Leon at all, or why they were picking on me. Our families used to be friends, but that was a long time ago, before my father died and theirs went to jail. Johnny and Leon think it was all my father's fault, as if their own dads couldn't have said no, even if my dad was the one who came up with the idea. So they're mean to me, because my father isn't around anymore for them to blame.

It was harder to ignore them the week the satellites were down. Mom's bosses were checking up on her a lot more, because their handhelds weren't working either. We got calls at home every night to make sure she was really there, and when she was at work, somebody had to go with her if she even left the building. Just like the old days, before the handhelds. And God only knew what David was up to. I guess he was still going to his warehouse job, driving a forklift and moving boxes around, because his boss would have called the probation office if he hadn't shown up. But he wasn't coming home when he was supposed to, and every time he did come home, he and Mom had screaming fights, even worse than usual.

So I had five days of not knowing where Bobo was, while Johnny and Leon baited me at school and Mom and David yelled at each other at home. And then finally the satellites came back online on Friday. The GPS people had been talking about how they might have to knock the whole system out of orbit and put up another one—which would have been a mess—but finally some earthside keyboard jockey managed to fix whatever the hackers had done.

Which was great, except that down here in Reno it had been snowing for hours, and according to the GPS, I was going to have to climb 3,200 feet to reach Bobo. Mom came in just as I was stuffing some extra energy bars in my pack. I knew she wouldn't want me going out, and I wasn't up to fighting with her about it, so I'd been hoping the snow would delay her for a few hours, maybe even keep her down in Carson overnight. I should have known better. That's what Mom's new SUV was for: getting home, even in shitty weather.

She looked tired. She always looks tired after a shift.

"What are you doing?" she said, and looked over my shoulder at the handheld screen, and then at the topo map next to it. "Oh, Jesus, Mike. It's on top of Peavine!"

I could smell her shampoo. She always smells like shampoo after a shift. I didn't want to think about what she smells like before she showers to come home.

"*He's* on top of Peavine," I said. "Bobo's on top of Peavine."

Mom shook her head. "Honey—no. You can't go up there."

"Mom, he could be *hurt*! He could have a broken leg or something and not be able to move and just be lying there!" The signal hadn't moved at all. If it had been lower down the mountain, I would have thought that maybe some family had taken Bobo in, but there still weren't any houses that high. The top of Peavine was one of the few places the developers hadn't gotten to yet.

"Sweetheart." Mom's voice was very quiet. "Michael, turn around. Come on. Turn around and look at me."

I didn't turn around. I stuffed a few more energy bars in my pack, and Mom put her hands on my shoulders and said, "Michael, he's dead."

I still kept my back to her. "You don't *know* that!"

"He's been gone for five days now, and the signal's on top of Peavine. He has to be dead. A coyote got him and dragged him up there. He's never gone that high by himself, has he?"

She was right. In the year he'd had the transmitter, Bobo had never gone anywhere much, certainly not anywhere far. He'd liked exploring the neighbors' yards, and the strips of wild land between the developments, where there were voles and mice. And coyotes.

"So he decided to go exploring," I said, and zipped my pack shut. "I have to go find out, anyway."

"Michael, there's nothing to find out. He's dead. You know that."

"I do *not* know that! I don't know anything." *Except that David's a piece of shit.* I did turn around, then, because I wanted to see her face when I said, "He hasn't been home since Monday, Mom, so how do I know what's happened? I haven't even *seen* him."

I guess I was up to fighting, after all. It was an awful thing to say, because it would only remind her of what we were all trying to forget, but I was still happy when she looked away from me, sharply, with a hiss of indrawn breath. She didn't curse me out, though, even though I deserved it. She didn't even leave the room. Instead she looked back at me, after a minute, and put her hands on my shoulders again. "You can't go out there. Not in this weather. It wouldn't even be safe to take the SUV, or I'd drive you—"

"He could be lying hurt in the snow," I said. "Or holed up somewhere, or—"

"Michael, he's dead." I didn't answer. Mom squeezed my shoulders and said gently, "And even if he *were* alive, you couldn't reach him in time. Not all that way; not in this weather. Not even in the SUV."

"I just want to know," I said. I looked right at her when I said it. I wasn't saying it to be mean, this time. "I can't stand not knowing."

"You do know," she said. She sounded very sad. "You just won't let yourself know that you know."

"Okay," I told her, my throat tight. "I can't stand not seeing, then. Is that better?"

She took her hands off my shoulders and sighed. "I'll call Letty, but it's not going to do any good. Is your brother home?"

"No," I said. David should have been home an hour before that. I wondered if he even knew that the satellites were back up.

Mom frowned. "Do you know where he is?"

"Of course not," I said. "Do you think I care? Call the sheriff's office, if you want to know where he is."

Mom gave me one of her patented warning looks. "Michael—"

"He let Bobo out," I said. "You know he did. He did it on purpose, just like all the other times. Do you think I care where the fuck he is?"

"I'm going to go call Letty," Mom said.

David hated Bobo the minute we got him. He was my tenth birthday present from Mom and Dad. The four of us went to the pet store to pick him out, but when David saw the kittens, he just wrinkled his nose and backed up a few feet. David was always doing things like that, trying to be cool by pretending he couldn't stand the rest of us.

David and I used to be friends, when we were younger. We played catch and rode our bikes and dug around in the dirt pretending we were gold miners, and once David even pulled me out of the way of a rattlesnake, because I didn't recognize the funny noise in the bushes and had gone to see what it was. I was six then, and David was ten. I'll never forget how pale he was after he yanked me away from the rattling, how scared he looked when he yelled at me never, *ever* to do that again.

The four-year difference didn't matter back then, except that it meant David knew a lot more than I did. But once he got into high school, David didn't want anything to do with any of us, especially his little brother. And all of a sudden he didn't seem so smart to me anymore, even though he thought he was smarter than shit.

I named my new kitten Bobcat, because he had that tawny coat and little tufts on his ears. His name got shortened to Bobo pretty quickly, though, and that's what we always called him—everybody except David, who called him "Hairball." By the time Dad died, Bobo was a really big cat: fifteen pounds, anyway, which was some comfort when David started "accidentally" letting Bobo out of the house. I figured he could hold his own against most other cats, maybe even against owls. I tried not to think about cars and coyotes, and people with guns.

He started going over the fence right away, but he was good about coming home. He always showed up for meals, even if sometimes he brought along his own dessert: dead grasshoppers, and mice and voles, and once a baby bird. Dr. Mills says that when cats bring you dead prey, it's because they think you're their kittens, and they're trying to feed you.

Bobo was a good cat, but David kept letting him out, no matter how much I yelled at him about it. Mom tried to ground David a couple of times, but it didn't work. David just laughed. He kept letting Bobo out, and Bobo kept going over the fence. It took me four months of allowance, plus Christmas and birthday money, to save up enough for the transmitter chip and the handheld. David laughed about that, too.

"He's just a fucking *cat*, Mike. Jesus Christ, what are you spending all your money on that transmitter thing for?"

"So I can find him if he gets lost," I said, my stomach clenching. Even then, I could hardly stand to talk to David.

"If he gets lost, so what? They have a million more cats at the pound."

And you'd let them all out if you could, wouldn't you? "They don't have a million who are mine," I said, and Mom looked up from chopping onions in the kitchen. It was one of her days off.

"David, leave him alone. You're the one who should be paying for that transmitter, you know." And they got into a huge fight, and David stomped out of the house and roared off in his rattletrap Jeep, and when all the dust had settled, Mom came and found me in my room. She sat down on the side of the bed and smoothed my hair back from my forehead, as if I was seven again instead of thirteen, and Bobo jumped down from where he'd been lying on my feet. He'd been licking the place where Dr. Mills had put the transmitter chip in his shoulder. Dr. Mills said that licking would help the wound heal, but that if Bobo started biting it, he'd have to wear one of those weird plastic collars that looks like a lampshade. I hadn't seen him biting it yet, but I was keeping an eye on him. When Mom sat on the bed, he resettled himself under my desk lamp, where the light from the bulb warmed the wood, and went back to licking.

Bobo always liked warm places. Dr. Mills says all cats do.

Mom stroked my forehead, and watched Bobo for a little while, and then said, "Michael—sometimes you can know exactly where people are, and still not be able to protect them." As if I didn't know that. As if any of us had been able to protect Dad from his own stupidity, even though the pit bosses knew exactly where he was every time he dealt a hand.

I knew Mom was thinking about Dad, but there was no point talking about it. Dad was gone, and Bobo was right in front of me. "I'd keep him inside if I could, Mom! If David—"

"I know," she said. "I know you would." And then she gave me a quick kiss on the forehead and went downstairs again, and after a while, Bobo got off the desk and came back to lie on my feet. Watching him lick his shoulder, I wondered what it felt like to have a transmitter.

I'm the only one in the family who doesn't know.

Letty's Mom's best friend; they've known each other since second grade. Letty works for the BLM, and they have really good topo maps, so she could tell me exactly where Bobo was: just inside the mouth of an abandoned mine.

"He could have crawled there to get out of the snow," I said. The transmitter signal still hadn't moved. Mom and Letty exchanged looks, and then Mom got up.

"I'm going upstairs now," she said. "You two talk."

"He *could* have," I said.

"Oh, Michael," Mom said. She started to say something else, but then she stopped. "Talk to Letty," she said, and turned and left the room.

I listened to Mom's footsteps going upstairs, and after a minute Letty said, "Mike, it's not safe to go out there now. You know that, right? It wouldn't be safe even in a truck. Not in this weather. And in the snow, you can know exactly where something is and still not be able to get at it."

"I know," I said. "Like that hiker last year. The one whose body they didn't find until spring." Except that the hiker hadn't had a transmitter, so they hadn't known where he was. It didn't matter. For ten days after he went missing, the cops and the BLM had search teams and helicopters all over the mountain, and never mind the weather.

"Yes," Letty said, very quietly. "Exactly." She waited for me to say something, but I didn't. "That guy was dying, you know. He was in a lot of pain all the time. His wife said later she thought maybe that was why he went out in a storm like that, while he could still go out at all."

Letty stopped and waited again, and I kept my head down. "He went out in bad weather," she said finally, "near dark. It's snowing now, and you were getting ready to hike up the mountain when your mom got home at seven-thirty. Michael?"

"Bobo could still be alive," I said fiercely. "It's not like anybody else *cares*. It's not like the state's going to spend thousands of dollars on a search and rescue!"

"So you were thinking—what?" Letty said. "That you'd go up there and get everybody hysterical, and get a search going, and while they were at it, they'd bring Bobo back? Was that the plan?"

"No," I said. I felt a little sick. I hadn't thought about any of that. I hadn't even thought about how I was going to get Bobo back down the mountain once I found him. "I just—I just wanted to get Bobo, that's all. I thought I could go up there and it would be okay. I've hiked in snow before."

"At night?" Letty asked. Then she sighed. "Mike, you know, a lot of people care about Bobo. Your mom cares, and I care, and Rich Mills cares. He was a sweet cat, and we know you love him. But we care about you, too."

"I'm fine," I told her. I wasn't sitting in the mouth of a mine during a snowstorm. I wasn't registered with the sheriff's office.

"You wouldn't be fine if you went up on Peavine tonight," Letty said. "That's the point. And even if Bobo's still alive—and I don't think he can be, Michael—you can't help him if you're frozen to death in a gully somewhere. Okay?"

I stared at the handheld, at the stationary signal. I thought about Bobo huddled in the mouth of the mine, getting colder and colder. He hated being cold. "Is it true that when you freeze to death," I said, "you feel warm at the end?"

"That's what I hear," Letty said. "I don't plan to test it."

"I don't either. That wasn't what I meant."

"Good. Don't do anything stupid, Mike. Search and rescue might not be able to get you out of it."

I felt like I was suffocating. "I was putting food in my pack. An entire box of energy bars. Ask Mom."

Letty shrugged. "Energy bars won't keep you from freezing."

"I *know* that."

"Good. And one more thing: don't you pay any mind to those Schuster and Flanking kids. They're slime."

I jerked my head up. How did she know about that? She raised an eyebrow when she saw my face, and said, "People talk. Folks at my office have kids in your school. The bullies are slime, Michael, and everybody knows it. Don't let them give you grief. Your mother's a good person."

"I know she is." I wanted to ask Letty if she'd told Mom about Johnny and Leon, wanted to beg her not to tell Mom, but the way adults did things, that probably meant that telling Mom would be the first thing she'd do.

Letty nodded. "Good. Just ignore them, then."

It was easy for her to say. She didn't have to listen to them all the time. "That wasn't why I was going out," I told her. "I was going after Bobo."

"I know you were," Letty said. "I also know nothing's simple." She folded her topo map and stood up and said, "I'd better be getting on home, before the weather gets any worse. Tell your Mom I'll talk to her tomorrow. And try to have a good weekend." She ruffled my hair before she went, the way Mom had when Bobo got the chip. Letty hadn't done that since I was little. I didn't move. I just sat there, looking at the blip on the handheld.

After a while I went up to my room. David hadn't come back yet, not that I cared, and Mom's door was closed. I knew she was sleeping off the shift. I also knew she'd be out of bed and downstairs in two seconds if she heard David coming in or me going out. She'd hung the front and back doors with bells, brass things from Nepal or someplace she'd gotten at Pier One. You couldn't go out or come in without making a racket, and you couldn't take the bells off the door without making one, either. "You learn to sleep lightly when you have babies," Mom told me once, as if either me or David had been babies for years. And our windows were old, and pretty noisy in their own right. And it was snowing harder.

So I just sat on my bed and stared out the window at the snow, trying not to think. My window faces east, away from Peavine, towards downtown. I couldn't see the lights from the casinos because of the snow, but I knew they were there. After a while it stopped snowing, and a few stars came out between the clouds, and so did the neon: the blue and white stripes of the Peppermill, which stands apart from everything else, south of downtown, and the bright white of the Hilton a bit north of that—"the Mother ship," Mom always calls it—and then, clustered downtown, the red of Circus Circus and the green of Harrah's, which Mom calls Oz City, and the flashing purple of the Silverado, where Dad used to work.

Dad loved this view; he was so proud that we could look down on the city. He couldn't stop crowing about it to all his friends. I remember when he brought George Flanking and Howard Schuster, Leon and Johnny's dads, into my room so they could look out my window, too. So they could see "the panorama." That was what Dad called it. We'd never been able to see anything from our old windows, except more trailers across the way. "I'm going to get us out of this box," Dad said when we lived there. "We're going to live in a real house, I swear we are." And then we moved here, to a real house, and pretty soon that wasn't big enough for him, either.

I shut my blinds and flopped down on my bed. Someplace a dog had started to bark, and then another joined in, and another and another, until the whole damn neighborhood was going nuts. And then I heard what must have set them off: the yipping howl of a coyote, trotting between houses looking for prey.

When we bought our house five years ago, the street ended a block from here, and that was where the mountain started. Winter mornings, sometimes, we'd see coyotes in our driveway. Now the developers have built another hundred houses up the street, with more subdivisions going up all the time: fancy houses, big, the kind we could never afford, the kind that made Dad's eyes narrow, that made him spend hours hunched over his desk. The kind he talked about when he went out drinking with George and Howard, I guess. I don't know who's buying those big houses; casino and warehouse workers can't afford places like that. Mom could, maybe, if she weren't saving for nursing school. The only people I can think of who might live there are the ones who work for the development companies.

So we don't get coyotes in our driveway anymore, but they're still around. They travel in back of the houses, next to the six-foot fences people put around their yards. There's still sagebrush between the subdivisions, and rabbits, and you can still follow those little strips of wildness to the really wild places, up on the mountain.

Coyotes are unbelievably smart, and they'll eat anything if they have to, and it doesn't bother them when people cut the land into pieces. They like it, because the boundaries between city and wilderness are where rodents live, and rodents are about coyotes' favorite food, aside from cats. So when we cut things up for them, there are more edges where they can hunt. It doesn't hurt that we've killed most of the wolves, who eat coyotes when they can, or that coyotes look so much like dogs. They can sneak in just about anyplace. Dr. Mills says there are coyotes living in New York City now, in Central Park. There are millions of them, all over the country.

Ranchers and farmers hate them because they're so hard to kill, and because even if you kill them, there are always more. But I can't hate them, not even for eating cats. They're smart and they're beautiful, and they're just trying to get by, and as far as I can tell, they're doing a better job of it than we are. They know how to work the system. That's what Dad thought he was doing, but he wasn't smart enough.

I lay there, listening to that coyote and to all the dogs, still trying not to think, but thinking anyway: about what a weird town this is, where you get casinos and coyotes both, where the developers are covering everything with new subdivisions, but there's still a mountain where you can die. After a while it got quiet again, and I peeked out the window and saw more snow. A while after that I heard the bells jangling downstairs, and heard Mom's feet hitting her bedroom floor and thudding down the stairs. When she and David started yelling at each other, I pulled my pillow over my head and finally managed to go to sleep.

It wasn't snowing when I woke up on Saturday, but it looked like it might start again any minute. The transmitter signal still hadn't moved, and when I thought about Bobo out there in the cold, I felt my own heart freezing in my chest. I heard voices from downstairs, and smelled coffee and bacon. Mom and David were both home, then. I threw on clothing and grabbed the handheld and ran down to the kitchen.

"Good morning," Mom said, and handed me a plate of bacon and eggs. She was wearing sweats and looked pretty relaxed. David was wearing his bathrobe and scowling, but David always scowls. I wondered what he was doing up so early. "Any change on the screen, Mike?"

"No," I said. I knew she didn't think there ever would be, and I wondered why she'd asked. David's face had gone from scowling to murderous, but that was all right, because I planned to be out the door as soon as possible.

"Okay," Mom said. "We're all going up there after breakfast."

"We are?" I said.

"Your brother's coming whether he wants to or not, and I asked Letty to come too. Rich Mills has to work this morning. Unless you'd rather not have all those people, honey."

"It's okay," I said. So that's what David was doing up. Mom was making him come as punishment, so he could see what he'd done, and Letty was coming because she had the maps, and maybe to help Mom keep me and David apart if we tried to kill each other. And Mom wouldn't think it was important to have Dr. Mills there, because she didn't think Bobo was still alive. I put down my plate and gulped down some coffee and said, "I'm going to go put the carrying case in the SUV."

"You're going to eat first," Mom said. "Sit down."

I sat. Driving up Peavine in the snow wasn't exactly Mom's idea of a day off; the least I could do was not give her any lip. David bit into his toast and said around a mouthful of bread, "I'm not going."

That was fine with me, but I wasn't going to say so in front of Mom. It was their fight. "You're coming," she told him. "And if Bobo's still alive you're paying the vet bills, and if he's not, you're buying your brother another cat. And if we get another cat you'll damn well help us keep it in the house, or I'll call the sheriff's office myself and tell them to take you off probation and put you in jail, David, I swear to God I will!"

She would, too. Even David knew that much. He scowled up at her and said, "The cat didn't *want* to stay in the house."

"That's not the issue," Mom said, and I stuffed my face full of eggs to keep from screaming at David that he'd hated Bobo, that he'd wanted Bobo to die, and that I hoped he'd die, too: alone, in the cold.

I remembered one of the first times David had let Bobo out. Bobo didn't have the transmitter yet, and I was in the backyard calling his name. Suddenly I saw something race over the fence and he ran up to me, mewing and mewing, his tail all puffy. I picked him up and carried him inside and he stayed on my lap, with his face stuck into my armpit like he was hiding, for half an hour, until finally he calmed down and stopped shaking and jumped down to get some food. I'd hoped that whatever had spooked him so badly would keep him from wanting to go out again, even if David opened all the doors and windows, but I guess he forgot how scared he'd been. "He didn't want to freeze to death, either," I said.

David pushed his chair back from the table and said, "Look, whatever happened to your fucking cat, it's not my fault, and I'm not wasting my day off going up there." He looked at Mom and said, "Do whatever you want: it doesn't matter. I might as well be in prison already."

"Bullshit," Mom said. "If you go to prison, you'll lose a lot more than a Saturday. Do you have any idea how lucky you are not to be there already? Especially after the stunts you've been pulling this week?" Nevada's a zero-tolerance drug state, even for minors, so when David got caught driving stoned last year, with most of a lid of pot in the glove compartment of his Jeep, Mom had to use every connection she had to get him probation instead of jail. It would have been a "juvenile facility," since David was still a few weeks short of eighteen, but Mom says her connections said that wouldn't make much difference. Juvenile facilities are worse, if anything.

Mom didn't say who her connections are, and I don't want to know. Whoever they are, I figure they didn't help David entirely out of the goodness of their hearts. I figure they were scared of what Mom could tell people about them, even if what she does is legal.

"I told you," David said, "I've just been hanging out with some guys from work. You know: eating dinner, playing pool? I was in town."

"Right," Mom said. "And there's no way anybody could check that with the satellites down, is there? That's what you were counting on."

David rolled his eyes. "What time did the damn GPS go back up last night? Six-thirty or something? We were still eating then. We were at that pizza place in the mall. Call the sheriff's office and ask them, if you don't believe me." He jerked a thumb at my handheld and said, "How stupid do you think I am? I knew it could come back online any second. What, I'm going to take off for Mexico or something?"

Mom didn't bother to answer. She and I were the smart ones in the family: David took after Dad. Anybody stupid enough to get caught with that much pot was stupid enough to do just about anything else, as far as I could tell, but the only time I'd even started to say anything like that, right after his arrest, David had just glared at me and said, "Yeah, well, if you'd had to look at what I had to look at, you'd smoke dope too, baby brother."

As if I hadn't wanted to look. As if I hadn't kept trying to go outside. As if even now I didn't keep imagining what it had looked like, a million different ways, enough to keep me awake, sometimes.

But even then, I knew that David had only said it to make me feel guilty. He knew just how to get at everybody. Now he gestured at the handheld again and said bitterly, "I can't wipe my ass without those people knowing about it."

He was needling Mom, because that's what Dad had always said about dealing blackjack at the Silverado. The dealers were under surveillance all the time: from pit bosses, from hidden cameras. "You can't get away from it," Dad said. "It's like working in a goddamn box, with the walls closing in on you." But Dad chose his box, and so did David.

"That's not the issue," Mom told David again. "It's more than staying in county limits, David. You're supposed to come home straight after work. You know that."

"So you're my jailor now? Just like the casino was Dad's and the Lyon County cops are—"

"Stop it," Mom said, her voice icy. "I'm not your jailor. I'm the one who kept you out of jail. You agreed to the terms of the probation!"

"Like you agreed to all those terms when you decided to go down to Carson and play *nurse*?"

Mom was out of her chair then, and David was out of his, and they stood nose to nose, glaring at each other, and I knew that there was no way we were all going up on Peavine today, because they wouldn't be able to sit in the same car even if David had wanted to go, even if I'd wanted him there. Nothing David says to Mom ever makes any real sense, but he knows exactly how to get to her. Sometimes he has to keep at it for a while, but Mom always snaps eventually, even if the same thing has happened a million times before. Just like Bobo being scared by something outside, and still going out again when David gave him the chance. David knows exactly how to get people to hurt themselves.

They were still eye to eye, like cats circling each other before a fight, when the doorbell rang. "I'll get it," I said. Maybe it was Letty, and I could warn her about what was happening before she came inside.

It was a cop. "Good morning, son," he said. "I'm looking for David. That your brother?"

"Yeah," I said, but my legs felt like wood, and I didn't seem to be able to get out of the way.

"Don't worry," he said. "It's just a routine drug test."

That was supposed to happen on Fridays. So David had skipped his drug test, too. My stomach shriveled some more. "Will he have to go to jail?" I said. The house would be a lot quieter if David was in jail, but school would be worse. If David went to jail, he'd probably be in the same place as George Flanking and Howard Schuster, and I didn't want to think too much about that.

The cop's face softened. "No. Not if he's clean. He'll get a warning, that's all."

And then Mom, behind me, said, "Michael, let him *in,*" and my legs came alive and I got out of the doorway, fast, and the cop came in, tipping his hat to Mom.

"Morning, ma'am." I wondered if Mom was remembering the last time the cops were at our house. I wondered if this cop was one of her connections. I wonder that about all kinds of people: my teachers and all the cops and storekeepers and Dr. Mills, even. I hate wondering it, but that's another thing I can't talk to Mom about. It would just hurt her. It would just make me like David, or like Aunt Tina, who hasn't even talked to us since Mom started working down in Carson.

The fight Aunt Tina picked with Mom was as bad as any of David's: worse, maybe, because she doesn't even live with us. She wasn't even here when Dad died. It was none of her business. "Oh, Sherry! How can you do *that,* of all things? With your boys the ages they are, after what their father did? How will be they be able to hold their heads up, knowing—"

"Knowing that their mother's keeping a roof over their head? My secretarial job doesn't pay enough, Tina, not by itself—and if you know what else I can do to earn a hundred thousand a year, go right ahead and tell me!"

It was perfectly legal, and it would let Mom earn enough money to go to nursing school at UNR and get a job none of us would have to be embarrassed about. That's what she kept telling us. A year, she'd said, or two at the most. But it had already been two years, and she hadn't saved enough to quit yet, because the hundred thousand didn't include food or clothing or insurance, or all the tests Mom has to have to make sure she's still healthy. She has drug tests, too. She gets more tests than David does, even though she's not a criminal and never did anything wrong, and she has to pay for all of hers. And when she's in Carson she can't go into a casino or a bar by herself, and she can't be seen in a restaurant with a man, and she has to be registered with the Lyon County Sheriff's Office—because technically, she's not in Carson at all. Her job's not legal in big towns: not in Reno, not in Vegas, not even in lousy little Carson City, the most pathetic excuse for a state capitol you ever saw. Mom has to work right outside Carson, in Lyon County, which is still plenty close enough to be convenient for her connections.

It used to be that the women at Mom's job couldn't even leave the buildings where they work without somebody going with them, but now they have transmitters, instead. And it used to be that they had to work every day for three weeks, living at the job, and then get one week off, but some of them got together and lobbied to change that, because so many of them were single mothers, and they wanted to be able to go home to their kids at night. But they still can't live in the same county where they work, which is why Mom has to commute between Reno and Carson. Highway 395's the only way to get down there, and those thirty-five miles can get really bad in the winter. That's why Mom had to buy the SUV. The SUV wasn't included in the hundred thousand, either.

Mom doesn't know that I know a lot of this. I've heard her and Letty talking about it, especially about all the tests. Letty's afraid Mom's going to get something horrible and die, but Mom keeps pooh-poohing her. "For heaven's sake, Letty; it's not like they don't have to wear condoms!"

I got out of the cop's way and tried not to think about him wearing a condom. It's hard not to get really mad at Dad whenever I think things like that. It's hard not to get even madder at David. He has it easier than Mom does, and it's not fair. She's not the criminal.

I followed the cop into the kitchen. Mom was chit-chatting about the weather and pouring him a cup of coffee; David was disappearing down the hall to the bathroom, carrying a little plastic cup. I looked at the drug kit, sitting on the table next to our half-eaten breakfasts. "Only takes two minutes," the cop told me, "and then I'll be out of here and leave you folks to your weekend. Ma'am, you mind if I take my jacket off?"

"Of course not," she said, and he did, and when I saw the gun in its holster I took a step back, even though of course the cop would be wearing a gun, all cops wear guns. Nearly everybody around here owns guns anyway, except us. And Mom bit her lip and the cop stepped back too, away from me, raising his hands. He looked sad.

"Hey, hey, son, it's all right. I'll put the jacket back on."

"You don't have to," I said, my face burning. "I'm going up to my room, anyway." I wanted to get out of there before David came back out of the bathroom with his precious bodily fluids. I didn't want to stand around and find out what the drug tests said. So I went upstairs, wondering if there was anybody in the entire fucking town who didn't know everything about anything that had ever happened to us.

I flopped down on my bed again, waiting for the jangle of bells that would mean the cop had left. It came pretty quickly, and then there was another right after it, and I didn't hear any yelling, so I figured everything was okay. The phone had rung, somewhere in there. One of David's loser friends, maybe. Maybe he'd gone out. Maybe I wouldn't have to deal with him today. I wanted to be out on the mountain, climbing up to Bobo, but I knew the SUV would get there more quickly than I could, even with the delay.

But when I went back downstairs, David was in the living room watching TV and Mom and Letty were sitting at the kitchen table, looking worried. I looked at Mom and she said, "Relax. Your brother's clean."

"Okay," I said. She and Letty had probably been talking about me. "Are we leaving soon?"

Mom looked down at the table. "Michael, honey, I'm sorry. We can't leave right away. I'm waiting for a call from the doctor."

I squinted at her. "From the *doctor*?"

"I'm fine," Mom said. "It's nothing, really. She's looking at some test results, that's all, and I may need to take some antibiotics. But I don't want to miss the call. We'll go right after that, okay?"

"I'm going now," I said. *I thought they had to wear condoms.* "He's been up there since last night, Mom!"

Letty started to stand up. "Mike, I'll drive you—"

"You don't have to," I said. Right then, as much as I wanted to reach Bobo quickly, I wanted to be alone even more. "You can catch up with me after the doctor calls. Stay and talk to Mom." Stay and keep Mom and David out of each other's hair, I meant, and maybe Letty knew that, because she nodded and sat back down.

"Okay. We'll follow you as soon as we can. Be careful."

"Don't worry," I said. "It's not like you don't know where I'm going."

It felt good to be out, away from Mom and David, where I could finally breathe again. I cut over to the wild strip on the edge of our subdivision and started working my way up, past the new construction sites where the dump trucks and jackhammers were roaring away, even on Saturday, up to where all the signs say Bureau of Land Management and National Forest Service. The signs don't mean much, because the Forest Service and the BLM can sell the land to developers anytime they want. Right now, though, the signs meant that I was on the edge of wildness stretching for miles, all the way to Tahoe.

When the construction noises faded, I started hearing the gunfire. Shooters come up on Peavine for target practice; you can always find rifle shells on the trails, and there are all kinds of abandoned cars and washing machines and refrigerators that people have hauled up here and shot into Swiss cheese. Sometimes the metal has so many holes you wonder how it holds its shape at all. "Redneck lace," Dad used to call it—Dad who'd grown up in a trailer, and was so proud that he'd gotten us out of one: Dad who couldn't stand being called a redneck, even though he came up on Peavine every weekend with George Schuster and Howard Flanking, so they could drink beer and shoot skeet.

After he died, I couldn't come up on the mountain for a long time. But gunfire's one of those things you can't get away from here, any more than you can avoid new subdivisions, and Peavine's the only place I can come to be alone, really alone. I can hike up here for hours and never see anybody else. The gunfire's far away, and nearby are sagebrush and rabbits and hawks. In the summer you see lizards and snakes, and in the winter, in the snow, you see the fresh tracks of deer and antelope. I've seen prints that looked like mountain lion; I've seen prints that looked like dog, but were probably coyote.

I hiked hard, pushing myself, taking the steepest trails. It takes me three hours to get to the top of Peavine in good weather, and today I wanted the most direct route I could find. When you're slogging up a fifteen percent grade in the snow, it's harder to think about how miserable your cat would be, stuck up here in weather like this, and it's harder to think about what you want to do to your brother for letting him out. It's harder to think about who you know might be wearing condoms, or how condoms can break even when they're used right. It's harder to think about how angry you are that your mother's connections don't have to be tested before she is, to make sure she doesn't catch anything.

Mom never lied to me. She wouldn't say "some antibiotics" if she really meant "years of AIDS drugs." She wouldn't say it was nothing if she was scared she might be infected with something that could kill her. I was angry anyway, because nothing was fair.

So that fifteen percent grade was just what I needed. If Mom and Letty followed me, they'd be coming the easy way, up the road. They'd probably be angry if they couldn't find me, but they'd also get to the mine before I did, and they'd be able to drive Bobo back down. I hadn't been able to bring the carrying case with me, but I wouldn't be able to get it back down the mountain with Bobo in it anyway, not by myself. I hoped Mom had remembered to put the carrying case in the SUV. I hoped Bobo would still be in any kind of shape to need the carrying case at all.

I'm sorry, I told him as I climbed. *I'm sorry I didn't come after you sooner. I'm sorry I couldn't protect you from David. I'm sorry about whatever scared you. Bobo, please be alive. Please be okay.*

After a while, it started to snow. I kept going. I was wearing my warmest thermals and I was covered in Gore-Tex, and I had enough food in the pack for three days. And if Mom and Letty drove up in the snow and couldn't find me because I'd come back down, they'd really start freaking. So I headed on up, except that as soon as I could, I cut over to the road. I didn't see any fresh tire marks, which meant they were still behind me. I tromped along, checking the GPS every once in a while to make sure the signal hadn't moved, and then I heard a horn and turned around and saw headlights.

It was Dr. Mills. "Hey, Mike. I drove by your house when I got off work, and your mom said you'd headed up here." I scrambled into his truck; he had the heater blasting, and it felt good. "I hope you don't mind that your mom didn't come. My old truck can take the wear better than that fancy Suburban she has, and there's only so much room in here."

There was still plenty of room in the front seat. I glanced back at the flatbed: Dr. Mills had brought a carrying case, but of course on the way down, we'd want to be able to have Bobo in front with us, where it was warm. The part about Mom could have meant just about anything, depending on whether it was his excuse or hers. If it was hers, she could have been hoping that Dr. Mills would run a male-bonding father-figure trip on me, or she could have still been waiting for the doctor to call, or she and Letty could have been trying to force David to stay

74

in the house somehow. Or all of the above. If it was his—I didn't want to think about what it meant for him to be saving wear on her SUV, or not wanting her in the truck at all. Dr. Mills is married. I didn't want to think about him driving down to Carson.

So I looked at the handheld again. "He's in an old mine up here," I said.

"Mmm-hmmm. That's what your mom told me. How long since he's moved?"

"Not since the satellites came back up," I said, and Dr. Mills nodded. He stayed quiet for a long time, and finally I said, "You think he's dead, don't you? That's what Mom thinks."

The snow was coming down harder now, the windshield wipers squeaking in a rhythm that kept trying to lull me to sleep. Dr. Mills could have told me he didn't want to go on; he could have turned around. He didn't do that. He knew I had to see as much as I could. "Michael," he said finally, "I've been a vet for fifteen years, and I've seen plenty of miracles. Animals are amazing. But I have to tell you, I think it would take a miracle for Bobo not to be dead."

"Okay," I said, trying to keep my voice steady.

"With coyotes," he said, "usually it's quick. They break the necks of their prey, the same as cats do with birds and mice. So unless Bobo got away for a few minutes and then got caught again, he wouldn't have suffered long."

"Okay," I said, and looked at my hands. I wondered how long it would take me to break David's neck, and how much I could make him suffer while I did it. And then I thought, there goes David again, making me want to do something stupid, something that would only mean I was hurting myself.

It took us ten more minutes to get to the mine, and by then the snow was coming down so hard that we could hardly see a foot ahead of the truck. We got out and started walking towards where the mine should have been, snow stinging our faces. It was really cold. I couldn't see anything but snow: no rocks, not even the scrubby pines that grow up here. And within about ten feet I realized that the mine entrance was completely buried, and that even if we'd been able to find it, we'd probably need to dig through five feet of snow to get to Bobo.

"Michael," Dr. Mills yelled into my ear, over the wind. "Michael, I'm sorry. We have to go back."

I tried to say, "I know," but my voice wouldn't work. I turned around and headed towards the truck, and when I was back inside it I started shivering, even when the heat was blasting again. I sat in the front seat, with the empty space between me and Dr. Mills where Bobo should have been, and shivered and hugged myself. Finally I said, "You get warm, just before you freeze to death. If the coyotes didn't kill him—or if he went up on his own—"

"He's not in pain," Dr. Mills said. "That's a cliché, isn't it? But it's true. Michael, wherever he is now, he doesn't hurt. I can promise you that." And then he started telling me about some poem called "The Heaven of Animals," where the animals remain true to their natures. The predators still hunt and exult over their kill, and their prey rise up again every morning, perfectly renewed, joyously taking their proper part in the chase.

I guess it's a nice idea, but all I could think about was Bobo, shivering, hiding his head under my arm because he was scared.

So we drove on down the mountain, and pretty soon the snow stopped coming down so hard, and when we got back down to the developments, there was hardly any snow at all. You could still hear the construction equipment, and gunfire far off. Maybe the target shooters had moved farther down to get away from the snow. Dr. Mills hadn't said anything for a while, but when we started hearing the guns, he looked over at me.

Don't, I thought. Don't say it. Don't say anything. Just take me home, Dr. Mills, please. Don't say it.

"I never told you," he said, very quietly, "how sorry I am about what happened to your dad."

I stared straight ahead, thinking about Bobo, thinking about the hiker who'd died on Peavine. I wondered how long it would take the snow to melt.

When Bobo was a kitten, Dad used to dangle pieces of string for him. He always dangled them just high enough so Bobo couldn't get at them, and he'd laugh and laugh, watching Bobo jump. "We're going to enter this cat in the *Olympics*," he said. "Look at him! He must've made three feet that time!"

Bobo had lots of toys he could play with anytime he wanted, balls and catnip mice and crumpled-up pieces of paper I'd toss on the floor for him. But the minute Dad dangled that string, he'd stop playing with the stuff he could catch and go after the thing he couldn't have.

"Just like you," Mom always told him, watching them. "Just like you, Bill, jumping at what you'll never be able to get."

"Aw, now, Sherry! Why can't we have a Lexus? Why can't we have one of those fancy home theaters, huh?"

I thought he was kidding. Maybe Mom did, too.

When Dr. Mills dropped me off at home, David was gone, which was a good thing, because I don't know what I would have done if I'd had to look at him. Mom and Letty were still there. They tried to talk to me.

I didn't want to talk. I went straight up to my room and took off all the Gore-Tex and went to bed. I didn't want to think about what we didn't need anymore: the toys and the litter box and Bobo's food and water bowls. I knew I'd have to throw it all away. Mom had told David he had to get me another cat, but how could I get another cat? David would just let it out again. When I got into bed, I remembered that the handheld was still in my jacket pocket, and somehow that hurt more than anything else. I pulled my pillow over my head and turned my face to the wall. The pillow blocked out a lot, but I still heard the phone, and I still heard the jangling bells when Letty left, and I still heard them again when David came in. I couldn't block out the sounds of him and Mom yelling at each other, no matter how hard I tried.

I got up and tried to do homework, but that just made me think about how I was going to have to go to school on Monday morning. I tried to read, but all the words seemed flat and tasteless, like week-old bread. So finally I just sat on my bed, staring out at the casinos. They looked so small from here, little boxes you could pick up and throw like dice. And then I heard a coyote, off in the other direction.

Being good is one of the smallest boxes there is: Mom knows that, and so do I, and so did Dad. Mom was the only one who never complained about it, but what did I know? Maybe she hated it as much as I did. I didn't see how she could like it. Maybe she felt like Dad said he'd always felt, like the walls were closing in on her. "If I could just get outside," he always told me. "Working in that damn casino, no daylight anywhere, all those people watching you all the time, you just want to go outside and take a walk, Mike, you know what I mean?"

After Dr. Mills drove me up to the mine, I knew what Dad meant. I sat there with the walls closing in on me, and I couldn't breathe. I needed more room. I wanted to be outside with the coyotes, running around the outside of the boxes, invisible. Even if you try to watch a coyote to see what it's doing, even if you try to track it, it will disappear on you. It will fade into the grass, into the sagebrush, into shadows. And you'll know that wherever it is, it's laughing.

Sunday was quiet. David stayed in front of the TV, and I finally got my homework done, and Mom cleaned the house, humming to herself while she worked. She had to be on antibiotics for ten days, and she couldn't work until the infection was gone. "Ten-day vacation," she told me cheerfully, but she didn't get paid vacations any more than she got anything else. All it meant was ten days' pay out of the nursing-school fund.

Once I asked her what would happen if the Lyon County sheriff's office saw her transmitter signal outside the building where she works. What if they tracked it and found her in a bar, or in a casino, or in a restaurant with a man? Would she go to jail?

She'd shaken her head and said very gently, "No, honey, I'd just lose my job. And I'd never do that, because it would be stupid." Because it would be like what Dad did, she meant. "Don't worry."

When I got up on Monday morning, my stomach hurt already. I hadn't been able to sleep very well, because I kept thinking about Bobo buried in the snow. I kept wondering about what I hadn't been able to see, worrying that maybe there'd been some way to save him and I hadn't figured it out.

I couldn't stand the idea of going to school. I couldn't stand facing Johnny and Leon; I couldn't stand the idea of going through all that and not being able to come home and have Bobo comfort me, curling up on my stomach the way he always did to get warm. I'd always been able to tell Bobo everything I couldn't talk about to anybody else, and now he was gone.

But I had to go to school, so I wouldn't upset Mom.

I had an algebra test first period. I knew the material; I could have done all the problems, but I couldn't make my hands move. I just sat there and stared at the paper, and when Mrs. Ogilvy called time, I handed it in blank.

She looked at it, and both her eyebrows went up. "Michael?"

"I didn't feel like it," I said.

"You didn't—Michael, are you sick? Do you want to go to the nurse?"

"No," I said, and walked away, out into the hall, to my next class, which was English. We were talking about Julius Caesar. I sat against the back wall and fell asleep, and when the bell rang I got up and went to Biology, where we were dissecting frogs. Biology was always bad, because Johnny and Leon were in there. They grabbed the lab station next to mine, and whenever they thought they could get away with it they whispered, "Hey, Mike, know what we're gonna do after school? Hey, Mike—we're gonna drive down to Carson. We're gonna drive down to Carson *and fuck your mother!*"

Donna Mauro, my lab partner, said, "They are *such* jerks."

"Yeah," I said, but I couldn't even look at Donna, because I was too ashamed. I knew everybody in school knew what my mother did, but that didn't mean I liked it when Johnny and Leon reminded them. I wondered if one of Donna's parents worked for the BLM and had talked to Letty, but it could have been just about anybody.

I stared down at the frog. We were supposed to be looking for the heart. I pretended it was Johnny instead, and sliced off a leg. Then I pretended it was Leon, and sliced off the other leg.

Donna just watched me. "Um, Mike? What are you doing?"

"I thought I'd have frog legs for lunch," I said. My voice sounded weird to me, tinny. "Want one?"

"Um—Mike, that's cool, but we have to find the heart now."

I handed her the scalpel. "Here. You find the heart."

And then I turned and walked away.

It was really easy, actually. I just walked out of the room, like I had to go to the bathroom but had forgotten to ask permission. Behind me I could hear Mr. Favaro, our teacher, saying something, and Donna answering, but the voices didn't really reach me. I felt like I was inside a bubble: I could see outside, but everything was muffled, and no one could get inside. They'd just bounce off.

It was wonderful.

I walked along the hall, and Mr. Favaro ran up behind me, gabbling something. I had to listen really carefully to make out what he was saying. It sounded like he was on the moon. "Mike? Michael? Is there something you need to tell me?"

I considered this. "No," I said. If I'd been Leon or Johnny or one of the bad kids, Mr. Favaro probably would have yelled at me and told me to get back inside the room, *now,* but he was spooked because it was me acting this way. So he gabbled some more, and I ignored him, and finally he ran away in the other direction, towards the principal's office.

I just walked out the door. My jacket was back in my locker, but it was pretty warm out, at least in the sun, and I wasn't cold. The bubble kept me warm. I started walking down a gully that angled down past the football field. I could hear voices behind me; I didn't stop to try to figure out what they were saying. But then a van pulled up alongside the gully, and people got out, and the voices started again. "Michael. Michael Michael Michael Michael Michael."

"*What?*" I said. Ms. Dellafield was there, the principal, and Mr. Ambrose, the school nurse, and two guidance counselors whose names I could never remember. They all looked really scared. I blinked at them. "I just wanted to take a walk," I said, but they were in a semicircle around me, pushing at the edges of the bubble, herding me towards the van. "You don't have to do this," I told them. "Really. I'm fine. I was just taking a walk."

They didn't listen. They kept herding me towards the van, and then I was inside it, and the door was closing.

They drove me back to school, and then they herded me into Mr. Ambrose's office, and then Ms. Dellafield went to call Mom while Mr. Ambrose and the two guidance counselors stood there and watched me, like they were going to tackle me if I tried to move. "Why are you doing this?" I kept asking them. "I was just going for a walk." It didn't make any sense. I'd seen other kids walk out of classes: they'd never gotten this kind of attention. "I'll go back to biology, okay? I'll dissect my frog. You don't have to call my mother!"

And at the same time I thought, thank God Mom's home today. Thank God she's not down in Carson, so that Ms. Dellafield doesn't have to hear them say whatever they say when they answer the phone there, not that there's any chance that Ms. Dellafield doesn't know where Mom works, since everybody else knows it. But even all that didn't bother me as much as usual, because the bubble was still basically holding. Mr. Ambrose and the guidance counselors kept asking me how I was, and I kept telling them I was fine, thank you, and how are all of you today? And they kept looking more and more worried, as if I'd answered them in another language, one where "fine" meant "my eyeballs are about to explode." So I sat there feeling fine, if a little far away, and thinking, these people are really weird.

And finally, after about half an hour, I heard voices outside Mr. Ambrose's office, and then the door opened and Mom came in. She was leaning on David. David had his arm around her, and he was really pale. It was the same way he'd looked after he pulled me away from the rattlesnake.

I squinted at him and said, "What are *you* doing here? What happened?"

"She called me," David said. He sounded like he was choking. "At work. When they called her. So we could come over here together."

I looked at Mom. She was crying, and then I got really scared. "What's going on?" I said. "Mom, what's wrong? Are you okay? Did something happen to Letty?" Maybe Mom had called Ms. Dellafield and said something had happened and they had to find me. But that wouldn't explain the van and the guidance counselors, would it? If something had happened to Letty, wouldn't Mom have driven over here to tell me herself?

Everybody just stared at me. Mom stopped crying, and wiped her eyes, and said very quietly, "Michael, the question is, are *you* okay?"

"I'm *fine*! Why does everybody keep asking me that? I was just going for a walk! Why doesn't anybody believe me?"

And Mom started crying again and David shook his head and said, "Oh, you stupid—"

"David." Ms. Dellafield sounded very tired. "Don't."

I felt like I was going crazy. "Would somebody please tell me what's going on? I was just—"

"Michael," Mom said, "that's what your father said, too."

I blinked. The room had gotten impossibly quiet, as if nobody else was even breathing. Mom said, "He said he was just going for a walk, and then he went out into the yard. Don't you remember?"

I looked away from all of them, out the window. I didn't remember that. I didn't remember anything that had happened that day, before the shot. It didn't matter: everyone else at school knew the story, and they'd remembered it for me. "I really was just going for a walk," I said, and then, "I don't even have a gun."

Ms. Dellafield said I should take the rest of the day off, so Mom and David and I drove home together, in David's jeep. When Ms. Dellafield called Mom at home, Mom had been too upset even to drive, so she'd called David and he'd left work and picked her up and driven her to school. He drove us all home, too. He drove really carefully. Once a squirrel ran into the road and David slowed down until it got out of his way. I'd never seen him drive like that before. And when we were walking into the house, Mom tripped, and David reached out to steady her.

The last time I'd seen Mom and David leaning on each other, they'd been coming in from the yard. I remembered that part. My ears had still been ringing, but Letty wouldn't let me go, no matter how hard I fought. She'd been eating lunch with us when it happened. "Let me see," I kept telling her, trying to break free. "Let me go out there! I want to see what happened!"

But Letty wouldn't let go, because the first thing that happened after the shot was that Mom and David ran out into the yard, and David started screaming, and then Mom yelled at Letty, "Keep Michael inside! Don't let him come out here!"

And they came back inside, and Mom called the police, and I kept saying, "I want to go see," and David kept shaking his head and saying, "No you don't, Michael, you don't want to see this, you really don't," and Letty wouldn't let go of me. And the cops came and asked everybody questions, and then Letty took me to her house, and by the time I got home, Mom and David had cleaned up the backyard, picked up all the little pieces of bone and brain, so that there was nothing left to see at all.

Dad was stupid. You can't beat the house: anybody who's ever been anywhere near a casino knows that. But he and George and Howard were trying. They'd worked out a system, the newspaper said; George or Howard, never both at once, would go in and play at Dad's table, and Dad would touch a cheek or scratch an ear, always a different signal, so they'd know when to double their bets. And then when they won, they'd split the take with him. They tried to be smart. They didn't do it very often, but it was often enough for the pit bosses and the cameras to catch on. And somehow, when Dad came home that day, he knew he'd been caught. He knew the walls were closing in.

George and Howard went to jail. I guess Dad knew he'd have to go there too. I guess he thought that was just too small a box.

Nobody said anything for a long time, after we got home from school. Mom started unloading the dishwasher, moving in little jerks like somebody in an old silent movie, and David sat down at the kitchen table, and I went to the fridge and got a drink of juice. And finally David said, "Why the hell did you do that?"

He didn't sound angry, or like he was trying to piss me off. He just sounded lost. And I hadn't been trying to do anything; I'd just been going for a walk, but I'd said that at least a million times by now and it was no good. Nobody believed me, or nobody cared. So instead I said, "Why did you keep letting Bobo out?"

And Mom, with her back to us, stopped moving; she stood there, holding a plate, looking down at the open dishwasher. And David said, "I don't know."

Mom turned and looked at him, then, and I looked at Mom. David never admitted there was anything he didn't know. He stared down at the table and said, "You kept saying you wanted to go outside. You kept—you were *fighting* to go outside. The cat wanted to go out, Michael. He did." He looked up, straight at me; his chin was trembling. "You didn't even have to look at it. It wasn't fair."

His voice sounded much younger, then, and I flashed back on that day when he saved me from the rattlesnake, when we were still friends, and all of a sudden my bubble burst and I was back in the world, where it hurt to breathe, where the air against my skin felt like sandpaper. "So you wanted me to get my wish by having to look at Bobo?" I said. "Is that it? Like I wanted any of it to happen, you fuckhead? Like—"

"Shhhh," Mom said, and came over and hugged me. "Shhhh. It's all right now. It's all right. I'm sorry. I'm sorry. David—"

"Forget it," David said. "None of it matters anymore, anyway."

"Yes it does," Mom said. "David, I made you do too much. I—"

"I want to go for a walk now," I said. I was going to scream if I couldn't get outside; I was going to scream or break something. "Can we just go for a walk? All of us? You can watch me, okay? I promise not to do anything stupid. Please?"

Mom and David have gotten along a lot better since then. Letty and I talked about it, once. She said they'd probably been fighting so much because David was mad at Mom for making him help her in the yard when Dad died, and Mom felt guilty about it, and didn't even know she did, and kept lashing out at him. And none of us were talking about anything, so it festered. Letty said that what I did at school that day was exactly what I needed to do to remind Mom and David how much they could still lose, to make them stop being mad at each other. And I told her I hadn't been trying to do anything, and anyway I hadn't even remembered what Dad had said before he went out into the yard. She said it didn't matter. It was instinct, she said. She said people still have instincts, even when they live in boxes, and that we can't ever lose them completely, not if we're still alive at all. Look at Bobo, she told me. You got him from a pet store. He'd never even lived outside, but he still wanted to get out. He still knew he was supposed to be hunting mice.

In June, when the snow melted from the top of Peavine, I hiked back up to the mine. I'd been back on the mountain before that, of course, but I hadn't gone up that high: maybe because I thought I wouldn't be able to see anything yet, maybe because I was afraid I would. But that Saturday I woke up, and it was sunny and warm, and Mom and David were both at work, and I thought, okay. This is the day. I'll go up there by myself, to see. To say goodbye.

All those months, the transmitter signal hadn't moved.

So I hiked up, past the developments, through rocks and sagebrush, scattering basking lizards. I saw a few rabbits and a couple of hawks, and I heard gunfire, but I didn't see any people.

When I got to the mine, I peered inside and couldn't see anything. I'd brought a flashlight, but it's dangerous to go inside abandoned mines. Even if it's safe to breathe the air, even if you don't get trapped, you don't know what else might be in there with you. Snakes. Coyotes.

So I shone the flashlight inside and looked for anything that might have been a cat once. There were dirt and rocks, but I couldn't even see anything that looked like bones. The handheld said this was the place, though, so I scrabbled around in the dirt a little bit, and played the flashlight over every surface the beam would reach, and finally, maybe two feet inside the mine, I saw something glinting in a crevice in the rock.

It was the chip: just the chip, a tiny little piece of silver circuitry, sitting there all by itself. Maybe there'd been bones too, for a while, and something had carried them off. Or maybe something had eaten Bobo and left a pile of scat here, with the chip in it, and everything had gone back into the ground except the chip. I don't know. All I knew was that Bobo was gone, and I still missed him, and there wasn't even anything that had been him to bring back with me.

I sat there and looked at the chip for a while, and then I put the handheld next to it. And then I went and sat on a rock outside the mine, in the sun.

It was pretty. There were wildflowers all over the place, and you could see for miles. And I sat there and thought, I could just leave. I could just walk away, walk in the other direction, clear to Tahoe, walk away from all the boxes. I don't have a transmitter. Nobody would know where I was. I could walk as long as I wanted.

But there are boxes everywhere, aren't there? Even at Tahoe, maybe especially at Tahoe, where all the rich people build their fancy houses. And if I walked away, Mom and David wouldn't know where I was. They wouldn't even have a transmitter signal. And I knew what that felt like. I remembered staring at the dark screen, when the satellites were offline. I remembered staring at it, and trying not to cry, and praying. *Please, Bobo, come back home. Please come back, Bobo. I love you.*

So I sat there for a while, looking out over the city. And then I ate an energy bar and drank some water, and headed back down the mountain, back home.

First published in *Asimov's Science Fiction Magazine,* May 2000.

ABOUT THE AUTHOR

Susan Palwick is an Associate Professor of English at the University of Nevada, Reno. She has published four novels, all with Tor-the most recent is 2013's *Mending the Moon*-and a story collection with Tachyon, *The Fate of Mice.* Her work has won the IAFA Crawford Award and the ALA Alex Award, and has been shortlisted for the World Fantasy and Mythopoeic Awards.

Shining Armor
DOMINIC GREEN

It was close to dawn. The sun was a sliver of brilliance just visible over the mass of canyons on the western horizon. There was no reason why the direction the sun rose in should not be arbitrarily defined as East; the only reason why the sun rose in the West on this planet was that, if looked at from the same galactic direction as Earth, it span retrograde. Even at this number of light years' distance, men still had an apron-string connecting them to their homeworld.

The old man was still doing his exercises.

The boy didn't realize why the exercises had to take so long. They didn't look hard to do, although when he tried to copy them, the old man laughed as if he were doing them in the most ridiculous manner possible. The old man used a sword while he did the exercises, but not even a real one—it had no edge, and was made of aluminum which could not even be made to take one. He held the sword-stick ridiculously, not even using his whole hand most of the time; usually he held it with only his middle finger and forefinger, some of the time with only the little and ring fingers. Both of his hands, in fact, were held in that peculiar crab claw, with the fingers separated.

Finally, though, there were signs that the old man was coming to the end of the set, stabbing around him to right and left with his stick. The boy now had something to do. Gradually, he scurried out among the rusting steel shells, carrying the basket of fruit. It was, of course, spoiled fruit, fruit the old man would not have been able to sell at market. There would have been no point in wasting saleable produce.

The boy arranged a marrow to the west, a pineapple to the east, a durian to the north, and a big juicy watermelon to the south. Each piece of fruit sat on its own square of rice paper. He was careful to leave the empty basket in a spot where it would not interfere with the old man's movements. Then, just as his elder and better was turning into his final movement, facing into the sun as it blazed up into the sky, the boy ran to the long half-buried shelf the old man called the dead hulk's 'glacis plate', and unwrapped the Real Sword.

The Real Sword was taller than he was. He had been instructed to unwrap it carefully. The old man had illustrated why by dropping a playing card onto the blade. The card had stuck fast, its weight driving the blade a good half centimeter into it.

The old man bowed to the sun—why? Did it ever bow back?—walked over to the sword, nodded stiffly to the boy, and picked up the weapon. He executed a few practice cuts and parries, jumping backwards and forwards across the sand. This was more exciting—he was moving quickly now, with a sword of spring steel.

Then, he became almost motionless, the sword whipped up into a position of readiness up above his head. As always, he was directly between all four pieces of fruit. Sometimes there were five pieces of fruit, sometimes six or seven.

The sword moved up and down, one, two, three, four times, the old man lashing out at all quarters, turning on his heel on the sand. There were four soft tearing sounds, but no sparks or sounds of metal hitting metal.

The old man stood finally upright, ready to slide the sword back into a nonexistent scabbard. He had lost the scabbard somehow years ago, nobody seemed to know how—nobody could convince him to shell out the money for a new one.

He walked over to inspect the fruit. All four pieces now lay in two pieces, making eight pieces. In all four cases, the cut had been deep enough to completely halve the fruit right down to the rind. In not one case had the rice paper underneath been touched. In some cases, the old man's activities had cut the rot clean out of the fruit. The boy gathered up the good pieces, which would now be breakfast.

The rotten pieces he slung away into the desert.

When they walked back toward the village, the General Alarm was sounding. This, the boy knew, could be very bad, as no alarm practice was scheduled for today.

General Alarm could mean that another boy like him had fallen down a melt-hole like a damned fool and the whole village was out looking for his corpsicle. Or it could mean that a flash flood was on the way and every homeowner had to rush out and bolt the streamliner onto the north end of his habitat, then rush back in and dog all the hatches. It might mean a flare had been reported, and everyone except Mad Farmer Bob who carried on digging his ditches in all weathers despite skin cancer and radiation alopoecia had to go underground till the All Clear.

But it was clear, when they reached the outskirts of the village, that this was none of these things. There was a personal conveyor in the Civic Square, with its green lights flashing to indicate it had been set to automatic guidance. Someone had used towing cable to secure three long irregular wet red shapes to the back of it, shapes the grown-ups would not let him see. But he had a horrible idea what they were, or what they had once been. Dragging your enemy behind a conveyor was a *badabing-badaboum* thing to do, and normally the boys in the village would have run and jostled to see such a marvelous sight. But when the men who had been dragged, probably alive, were Mr. d'Souza, big friendly Mr. d'Souza who had three hairy Irish wolfhounds, and Mr. Bamigboye, who told rude jokes about naked ladies, and even Mr. Chundi, who told kids to get off his property—then things did not seem so exciting.

Mr. d'Souza, Mr. Bamigboye, and Mr. Chundi were Town Councilors, and they had gone up to the Big City to argue with the authorities about the mining site. Although there was nothing there now but a few spray-painted rocks and prospectors' transponders, the boy knew that some Big City men had found rocks they called Radioactives upriver. But the boy's father said the Big City men were too lazy to dig the rocks out of the ground using shovels and the Honest Sweat Of Their Brow. Instead, they planned to build a sifting plant downstream of the village, and set off bombs also made of Radioactives in the regolith upstream. A handsome stream of Radioactives would thus flow downriver to the sifting plant, but the village's water would be poisoned. The villagers had all been offered what were described as 'generous offers' to leave by the Big City men; but the Town Councilors had voted to stay. The Big City men had been rumored to be hiring a top Persuasion Consultancy to deal with the situation. Now it seemed that the rumors had come true.

"We ought to take a few guns into town and sort out those City folk," said old father Magnusson, who thought everyone didn't know he ordered sex pheromones and illegal subliminal messaging software through the mail from Big City, but Aunt Raisa knew. Now no woman in town would either visit him or call him on the videophone.

"How many guns do we have? And small-bore ones, too, for seeing off interlopers, not armour-piercing stuff. The combine bosses will be protected by men in armour, ten feet tall, with magnetic accelerators that shoot off a million rounds through you POW-POW-POW before you pop your first round off! You are maximally insane." This was old mother Tho. Despite her insulting mode of communication, many of the older and wiser heads in the square were nodding their agreement.

"Don't be ridiculous," said Mother Murdo. "Magnetic accelerators are illegal."

"Anything illegal is legal if nobody is prepared to enforce the law. Have you not been up to the City recently? The mining combines have been making their own militaria for months. After they had to start making their own machine tools and coining their own money, weapons were the logical next step."

"But we are still citizens of the Commonwealth of Man," said father Magnusson, drawing himself up to his full one hundred and thirty-five centimeters, "and an attack on us would be an attack on the Commonwealth itself."

"Pshaw! The Commonwealth doesn't even bother to send out ships to collect taxes any longer," said mother Tho. "And when the taxman doesn't call, you *know* the government is in disrepair."

There were slow nods of appreciation from the crowd, most of whom were secretly glad that the tribute ships had not visited for so many years, but all of whom were alarmed at the prospect that those ships might have funded services whose unavailability might now kill the village.

"Well, in any case," said father Magnusson, "if they dare to come up *here* and attempt their person-dragging activities, the State will repel them instantly."

Mother Tho was unimpressed. "We must be pragmatic," she said. "The Guardian has not moved for sixty Good Old Original Standard Years. Not since the last Barbarian incursion."

Father Magnusson smacked his lips stolidly. "But I remember," he said, "when it last moved. And it operated most satisfactorily on that occasion. The Barbarians' ships filled the skies like locusts, but our Guardian was equal to them."

Mother Tho looked up into the sky, where the silhouette of the Guardian took a huge bite out of the sunrise. "Father, you are only one of perhaps two or three people still alive who remember the Guardian moving. And it is a machine, and machines rust, corrode, and biodegrade."

"The Guardian was built to last forever."

"But a Guardian also needs an operator. And where is ours?"

The old man put a hand upon the boy's shoulder, and moved away among the buildings before the conversation grew more heated.

• • •

"There are foreigners in the village," said the boy's mother, folding clothes with infinite precision. "Men from the mining company. They are asking for Khan by name, and you know why, old man."

The old man tucked the sword away in a crevice by the side of the atmosphere detoxifier. "Khan can look after himself."

"They had guns, by all accounts, and you know he can't." The boy's mother ran the iron over a fresh set of clothes. "Khan is fat and slow and has long since ceased to be any use in a fight. It isn't fair for him to be put through this." She looked up at the old man. "Something must be done."

The old man looked away. "They have heard the name Khan, heard that this Khan is the man who is our Guardian's operator. They perhaps mean harm. I will radio to Khan in the clear to stay out fixing watercourses and not return home until these men have gone. They will be listening, of course. This will inform them that their task is pointless, and then maybe they will leave."

"Or they will go out and search the watercourses till they find him."

"Khan knows the watercourses, and is more resourceful than you give him credit for. They will not find him."

"Khan is not as young as he once was. It will be cold tonight. You think that just because people are not as old as you, they are striplings who can accomplish anything."

"I think nothing of the sort, woman. Now boil me some water. I have a revitalizing tea to prepare for Mother Murdo's *fin-de-siècle ennui.*"

Khan's mother gathered up the heap of ironing and made her way out of the kitchen past the floor maintenance robot. "Boil your own water, and lower your underparts into it."

In order to defuse a family quarrel, the boy walked across the kitchen and turned on the water heater himself. He could not, however, meet the old man's eyes. Khan was, after all, his father.

The next morning, underneath the Guardian's metal legs, there was a gaggle of young men jostling for position.

"*I* will save the village!"

"You are wrong! It will be I!"

"No, I!"

The boy, who was running a flask of tea to Mother Murdo, saw Mother Tho rap three of them on the occiput with her walnut-wood staff in quick succession.

"Fools! Loblollies! What would you do, if you were even able to gain access to the Guardian's control cabin?" She pointed upward with her polyethylene ferrule at the ladder that led up the Guardian's right leg, with a dizzying number of rungs, up to the tiny hatch in its Under Bridge Area where a normal person's back body would be. Once, the boy had climbed all those rungs and touched the hatch with his hand for a bet, before being dragged down by his father, who told him not to tamper with Commonweal property. His father had had hair then, and much of it had been dark.

"If I gained access," swaggered the most audacious of the three, "I would march to the Big City and trample the mining syndicate buildings beneath boots of iron." And he blew kisses to those girls of marriageable age who had gathered to watch.

"*If* you gained access!" repeated the old witch, and grabbed him by the nose using fingers of surprising strength. "YOU WOULD NEVER GAIN ACCESS! Only the Guardian's operator has a key, and it is synchronized to his genetic code. You would do nothing but sit staring up at a big metal arse until the cold froze you off the ladder."

"OW! Bedder dat dan allow our iddibidual vreedods do be sudgugaded!" protested the putative loblolly.

Mother Tho let the young man go, and wiped her fingers on her grubby shawl.

"Our Guardian will defend us when its operator is ready," she intoned.

A voice chipped in across the crowd: "Our Guardian's operator is too feeble."

The boy shrunk back behind a battery of heat sinks and hid his face.

"It's true!" yelled another voice. "The company assassins turned out the whole of Mr. Wu's drinking establishment and threatened to shoot all its clientele one by one until Khan was turned over to them. In his confusion and concern for his customers, Wu turned over the wrong Khan, Khan the undertaker, and they killed him instantly. His tongue lolled out of his face like a frosted pickle. When the company men find the real Khan and kill him, there will be no trained professional to bury him."

"There are men in the village with guns?" said one of the bold youngsters, removing his thumbs from his belt, staring at his contemporaries with a face of horror.

"Ha!" gloated Mother Tho. "So our bravos are not quite so audacious when faced with the prospect of their skins actually being broken."

The boy put dropped his cargo of tea and ran for home.

Home proved to be more difficult to get to than usual. The boy followed the path most usually followed by children through the village, disregarding the streets and ducking under the support struts of the houses. Had crows been able to fly in this atmosphere instead of expiring exhausted after a few tottering flutters, he would have been traveling as the crow flew.

However, there was a problem. A small group of boys were holed up under the belly of Mother Tho's house, whispering deafeningly, fancifully imagining they were Seeing without Beeing Seen. But the boy was not afraid of other boys—at least, not as much as he was afraid of the men in the street who were tolerating Being Seen.

It was quite rare for children to be playing on the streets now. Their mothers were keeping them indoors. It was hoped that the Persuasion Consultancy assassins had not realized their mistake, and would be happy with having disabled the village's (admittedly one hundred per cent lethal) corpse-burying capabilities.

However, it seemed the assassins were not content with simple murder. They were standing in the street outside the house of Khan the undertaker, above which a grainy holographic angel flickered in the breeze. Not content with having murdered the undertaker's unburied corpse, the men had turned out the contents of his funeral emporium, headstones-in-progress and all, into the street. They were searching the whole pile of morbid paraphernalia with microscopic thoroughness, while his widow screamed and hurled such violent abuse as the poor woman knew. The boy could only conclude that onyx-look polymer angels were of great value to them.

"They are searching for our Guardian's access key," hissed one of the watchers in a strict confidence that carried all the way to the boy's ears.

"Only the Operator has the access key," said another boy. "Was Khan the Operator?"

"No," said a third. "I think it was Khan the farmer."

"Khan, a warrior! He is a fat little fruit seller."

"Operators are not chosen for their physical strength," said the third boy contemptuously. "The servomechanisms of the Guardian provide that. Operators are chosen for the extreme precision of their physical movements. It is said that the operator of the Guardian of the Gate of the City of Governance back on Earth was so precise in his motions that he was able to grip a normal human paintbrush between his Guardian's claws and inscribe the Rights and Duties of Citizens on the pavement in letters only three meters high."

The boy ducked under the hull of the nearest building and took a dog leg a habitat to the south before any Persuasion Consultancy men could engage him in conversation.

It was sunset. The sun was setting in the East.

The old man was sitting dozing, pretending to be absorbed in serious meditation. The boy walked up and pointedly slammed down the basket on a nearby ruined Barbarian war machine, pretending not to notice the old man starting as if he had been jumped on by a tiger.

"I have brought everything," said the boy. "Father is still at large. The assassins are reputed to be pursuing him along the north arroyo."

The old man nodded, and sucked his teeth in a repulsive manner. "Did you bring the weapons from underneath the loose slab in the conveyor garage?"

The boy nodded. "There is no need to conceal these weapons," he sniffed. "It is not illegal to possess them, and surely they can be of no intrinsic value."

The old man ran his hand along the bow as he lifted it from the bundle, and grinned. "There was also a picture of your grandmother underneath that slab," he said. "That is also of little intrinsic value."

"I never knew my grandmother," said the boy.

"Think yourself lucky," said the old man grumpily, "that *I* did." He set an arrow—the only arrow in the bundle—to the bow, and began trying to bend it, frowning as his hands shook with the effort.

"OLD MAN," called a voice. "STOP PLAYING AT SOLDIERS. WE DEMAND TO KNOW WHERE KHAN IS."

The bow collapsed. The arrow quivered into the dirt. The old man turned round. From the direction of the village, three young men, muscles big from digging ditches and lifting baskets, had strolled in to the clearing between the destroyed military machines. The boy realized with a sinking heart that he had been followed.

"My father," said their leader, "says that Khan is the operator of our Guardian."

The old man nodded. "True enough," he said.

"Then why is he hiding outside the village like a thief?" The youngster threw his hand out towards the horizon. "Not only are there murderers in our midst, but an army is gathering on our door-step. Employees of a Persuasion Consultancy engaged by the mining combine have arrived. They have delivered an ultimatum to the effect that, if the combine's generous terms are not accepted by sunrise tomorrow, they will evacuate the village using minimum force." He licked his lips nervously. "Scouts have been out, and the consultancy's definition of 'minimum force' appears to extend to fragmentation bombs and vehicle-seeking missiles."

The old man's face sunk into even more wrinkles than was normally its wont. "Khan," he said, "hides nowhere. Who here says that Khan hides?" And despite the fact that he was armed only with a bamboo bow and arrows, none of the young men present would meet his eyes.

"Father, we have the greatest respect for your age, and none of us would dare to strike a weak and defenseless old man. We simply wish to know when, if at all, our Operator intends to discharge his duty."

The old man nodded.

"Weak and defenseless, you say."

He slung out the bow at the spokesman of the group, who the boy believed was called Lokman. It whirled in the air and struck Lokman in the jaw. Lokman rubbed the side of his face, complaining bitterly; but still his manners were too correct to allow him to attack his elders.

"Pick the bow up," said the old man. He grubbed in the dirt for the arrow, and tossed it to Lokman. "Now notch the arrow, and pull the bow back as hard as you like." He did not rise from his sitting position.

Lokman shrugged, and heaved hard on the bow. It was an effort even for him, the boy noticed. The bow was almost as stiff as a roof-tie.

"Point the bow at me," said the old man, grinning. "You purulent stream of cat excrement."

Lokman's hands were shaking on the bow too now. It rotated round to point at the old man.

"Now fire!" said the old man. "*I said FIRE, you worthless spawn of a mining company executive—*"

"No, DON'T—" said the boy.

The string twanged free. The boy did not even see the arrow move. Nor did he see the old man's hand move. But when both hand and arrow blurred back into position, the one was in the other; and the hand held the arrow, rather than the arrow being embedded in the hand.

Lokman stared at the old man's hand for a second; then he snorted.

"A useful parlor trick," he said. "Can you do it against missiles?"

He threw down the bow and walked away.

"Khan is a coward who will not fight," he said, over his shoulder. "Besides, he could not get to the Guardian even if he wished. The assassins have the access ladder under guard. Pack up your things and leave, old man. The Councilors are leaving. We are *all* leaving. We are finished."

The old man watched the visitors leave. Then, he reached into the bundle, where a battered oblong of black plastic lay alongside the picture of the boy's grandmother. In the plastic were embossed the letters KHAN 63007248.

"It is good," said the old man. "You have made sure Khan has everything he needs."

The old man hung the oblong round his neck on a chain that pierced it, and felt his throat to make sure it was not visible as it hung.

"What time did they say the ultimatum expired tomorrow?" he asked, without looking at the boy.

"Sunup," said the boy.

"It is good," said the old man, nodding. "There is time. Run back to the village with these things, and return quickly. Then you shall accompany me while I deliver these troublemakers an ultimatum of our own."

"Why am I going with you?" said the boy.

"Because no man will shoot an old man," said the old man, "unless he is a wicked man indeed. But even a wicked man will not shoot an old man accompanied by a small boy—unless, of course, he is a *very* wicked man indeed." He grinned, and his grin was more gaps than teeth. "This, I must admit, is the only flaw in my plan."

Then he returned to his meditation, as if nothing had either happened or was about to. The boy seriously suspected he was sleeping.

The sun had set, and the reg had ceased to be its accustomed thousand shades of khaki. Now, it was the color of a world plunged underwater to a depth where every shade of anything became a democratic twilight blue.

The boy followed the old man uncertainly across the regolith towards a group of Persuasion Consultants lounging around an alcohol burner in the shadow of an APC. Even the burner's flame was blue, as if carefully coordinated to fit in with the night. The Consultants noticed the old man long before he began to jump up and down and wave his arms to get their attention, but the boy noticed that it was only at this point that they relaxed and began the laborious process of putting the safeties back on their weapons.

"Hey! Ugly Boy! Take me to your ugly leader!"

None of the Persuasion Consultants answered. Evidently none of them was willing to own up to the name of Ugly Boy.

"Suit yourselves, physically unprepossessing persons, but be informed that I bear a message from Khan."

The men began to fidget indecisively in their dapper uniforms. Eventually, one spoke up and said:

"If you are in communication with Khan, you must give us information on his whereabouts, citizen, or it will go poorly with you."

The old man scoffed. The boy was not entirely sure it was prudent to scoff in the presence of so much firepower. "You still do not know Khan's whereabouts? With the man right under your nose, and so many complex tracking systems in that khaki jalopy you are leaning against? For shame! Khan has a message for you. You must vacate the environs of this village, or as the appointed operator of the Guardian of this colony he will be obliged to make you quit by main force."

The spokesman crossed both hands over his rifle and said: "Your Guardian's operator is taking sides unjustifiedly in a purely civil matter, citizen. This is not a military matter. For this reason, Beauchef and Grisnez Incorporated regrets that, on behalf of its clients, it is forced to take action to eliminate this unruly operator, and that this action will continue until he himself quits the village. We are also making initial seismic surveys preliminary to placing charges underneath the Guardian's foundations, destroying the underground geegaws that charge it. Beauchef and Grisnez of course regret the damage to Commonwealth property concomitant to this strategy, but final blame for this unfortunate state of affairs must lie at the head of the operator concerned. That is *our* message, which you may convey to Khan."

The old man stood facing the line of soldiers silently for several seconds.

"Very well," he said. "Despite the fact that you behave like barbarians, you continue to describe yourselves as Commonwealth citizens and hence merit a warning in law; you have received that warning. Whatever consequences follow, Khan will not be answerable."

He said nothing more, but turned and trudged back in the direction of the village. There were sniggers from the line of riflemen.

In the morning, the boy's mother woke him well before dawn. She had already prepared sleeping gear for all of them, together with food she had irradiated that same morning. It would keep for a month, as well as making the boy's stomach turn when he ate it. This was the sort of food City people had to eat.

"But aren't we staying to defend the village?"

He got a slap for that one. Mother was in no mood to talk. She was crying softly as she walked round the rooms of the habitat, picking things up, putting things down, and the boy realized suddenly that she was deciding which of the pieces of her life she was going to take with her and which she was going to leave behind forever. He threw his arms around her, and this time she did not slap him.

"Go out and fetch the old one," she said. "Where is he? I've prepared the conveyor. We have to leave."

The boy told his mother that the old man had said he was going to do his exercises, and that, on this particular morning, the boy was not allowed to accompany him.

The boy's mother's eyes flew open in horror. She looked out of the window, which showed sand billowing down a dusty street.

She stood still a moment, as though paralyzed. Then she grabbed his arm.

"Come with me."

They walked out to the edge of the village. The village was small. It was not a long walk. Out there at the very edge of the sun farms, beyond a hectare or so of jet-black solar collectors, the wrecked battle machines of the Barbarians sat rusting in the sand.

What are Barbarians? the boy had asked his teacher once in class. And the answer had been quick and pat. Why, people from outside the Commonwealth, of course. *Any* people from outside the Commonwealth.

The machines sat at what the boy knew to have been the extreme limit of the Guardian's target acquisition range, sixty years ago.

Of the old man, there was no sign.

"Stupid old fool," said mother, and pulled the boy off down the village streets again. She seemed to know where she was going. Only two streets, two rows of gleaming aluminum habitats, and the old man came into view. Standing in the square at the Guardian's habitat-sized feet, he was arguing with a pair of Consultancy men, armored troopers holding guns that could track the electrical emissions of a man's heartbeat in the dark and shoot him dead through steel. He was carrying a sword.

"But I always do my exercises in the square at this time," the old man was saying, which was a lie.

"You are carrying a weapon, grandfather," said one of the Consultants gently, "which I am forced to regard as a potential threat, despite your advanced years."

The old man looked from hand to hand, then finally held up the sword as if he had only just realized it was there. "This? Why, but this is only an old sword-shaped piece of aluminum It cannot even be made to take an edge."

"All the same," said the Consultant persuasively, "out of deference to the tense situation in which we find ourselves, it would be safer if—"

"HOI!"

The shout broke the polite silence in the town square. Five heads turned towards it. As the sun heaved its head over the southern horizon, a figure staggered into town out of the desert. It waved its arms.

"HOI! It's me, Khan! Khan, the man you're looking for! Catch me if you can!"

Guns rose instantaneously to shoulders. Khan dived for cover. How useful that cover was was debatable, as a line of projectile explosions stitched its way across the wall of the nearest habitat like a finger tearing through tinfoil. When the guns had finished tracking across the building, the building was two buildings, one balanced precariously on top of the other, radiator coolant gushing from the walls and electrical connections sparking. Hopefully no-one was sitting headless at breakfast within it. The Consultancy men were already spreading out round the habitat, hoping to outflank their target if he had somehow survived the first attack. The boy's mother looked on, appalled.

Some caprice, however, drew the boy's attention upward.

The old man was on the inside leg of the metal colossus, on the access ladder, moving with dinosaurian slowness towards the Guardian's bumward access hatch.

The boy's jaw dropped.

Meanwhile, the men who were guarding the Guardian seemed on the point of following Khan and finishing him, until one of them remembered his orders, waved his comrade back to the square, pulled a communicator from one of his ammunition pouches, opened it, spoke into it, and flipped it shut again. Someone Else, he told his comrade, Could Do The Running. Up above, the old man was still moving, but with the speed of evolution, at the speed glass flowed down windowpanes, at the speed boys grew up doorposts. He had not even reached the knee. Surely, before the old fool reached the top of his climb, somebody in the village underneath had to notice? And what did he think he'd accomplish, if he once got up the ladder?

The two Consultants reassumed their positions underneath the Guardian's treads. They stood on the square of concrete, reaching all the way down through the regolith to the bedrock, that had been put there solely as a foundation for the vehicle to stand on. They faced outwards, willing to bleed good red blood to stop anyone who tried to get past them. One of them even remarked on the old man's sword discarded in the sand, saying that they Must Have Frit The Old Coot Away. Meanwhile, by pretending to scratch his eye against the dust, the boy was able to see, far above, the old coot pulling an battered slab of black plastic from his tunic and sliding it into what the boy knew, from the climb he had been dared to do a year ago, to be a recess in the circular ass-end access hatch about the same size as the slab. The hatch was also spraypainted with the letters AUGMENTED INFANTRY UNIT

MK 73 (1 OFF), and only members of the privileged club of boys who had taken the dare and made the climb knew it.

Something glittered like a rack of unsheathed blades in the Guardian's normally dull and pitted skin; the old man skimmed his fingers over the glitter rapidly, and the boy saw blood ooze out of his fingers onto the hatch cover momentarily, before the surface drank it like a vampire.

The key was tuned to the operator's genetic code. The vehicle had to have a part of him to know who he was.

The hatch slid into the structure, silently. The old man began to slip into the hole it had opened. But for all the wondrous silence of the mechanism, the old man was by now unable to prevent the boy's mother from standing with her head in the air gawping like a new-hatched chick waiting to be fed worms. And as she gawped, the guards gawped with her.

Luckily for the old man, the guards also took a couple of moments to do helpless baby chick impersonations before remembering they had weapons and were supposed to use them. The hatch had slid shut before they could get their guns to their shoulders, take aim and fire. They were not used to firing their weapons in that position, and the recoil, coming from an unaccustomed direction, blew them about on the spot like unattended pneumatic drills. The boy saw stars twinkle on the Guardian's hide. He was not sure whether they had inflicted any damage or not; the detonations left a mass of after-images on his retinas.

The two men could not have inflicted *too* much damage, however, as they thought better of continuing to shoot, and instead stood back and contemplated the crotch of the colossus.

For one long minute, nothing happened. The lead Consultant spoke quietly but urgently into his communicator, saying that he Wasn't Quite Sure Whether Or Not The Shit Indicator Had Just Risen to Nostril Deep.

Then the dust under the left tread of the Guardian moaned like a man being put to the press. The boy looked up to see the great pipe legs of the Augmented Infantry Unit buckling and twisting, as if the wind were blowing it off its base. But Guardians weighed so much they smashed themselves if they fell over, the boy knew; and despite the fact that the dry season wind howled down from the mountains here like a katabatic banshee, it had never stirred the Guardian as much as a millimeter from its post.

The Guardian was moving *under its own power.*

Huge alloy arms the weight of bridge spans swung over the boy's head. Knee joints that could have acted as railway turntables flexed arthritically in the legs. And at that point, the boy knew exactly who was at the controls of the Guardian.

The whole colossal thousand-tonne weapon was doing the old man's morning exercises. Moving gently at first, swinging its arms and legs under their own weight, cautiously bending and unbending its ancient joints. Some of those joints screamed with the pressure of the merest movement. The boy suddenly, oddly, appreciated what the old man meant when he talked of rheumatism, arthritis and sciatica.

The old man's exercises were good for a man with rheumatic joints who needed them oiling in the morning. But they were just as good for a village-sized automaton that had not moved for sixty standard years.

The men sent to guard the Guardian were backing away. From somewhere in the village on the other side of the buildings, meanwhile, someone else decided to fire at the machine. A pretty colored show of lights sprayed out of the ground and cascaded off the metal mountain's armour. Habitats that the cascade hit on the way back down became colanders full of flying swarf. The Guardian carried on its warm-up regardless.

Eight times for the leg-stretching exercise—eight times for the arm-swinging—eight times for the two-handed push up above the head—

The boy began to back away, and pulling at his mother's robe. He knew what was coming next.

Men ran out of the buildings with light anti-armour weapons. Many of the weapons were recoilless, and some argument ensued about whether they should really be pointed up into the sky or not. Some of them were loosed off at point blank range at the Guardian's treads, leaving big black stains of burnt hydrocarbon. But a Guardian's feet were among its most heavily armored parts. Every old person in town would tell you that. They were heavily armored because they were used to crush infantry.

The Guardian lowered its massive head to stare at the situation on the ground. The operator, the boy knew, was actually in the main chassis, and the head was only used to affix target acquisition systems and armament. That small movement of the head was in itself enough to make the Consultants back away and run.

One of the Consultants, thinking smarter than his colleagues, grabbed hold of the boy's mother, shouting at the sky and pointing a pistol shakily at her head. He might as well have threatened a mountain.

The Guardian turned its head to look directly at him.

The boy screamed to his mother to drop down.

The Guardian's hand came down like the Red Sea on an Egyptian. Or, the boy pondered, like a sword upon a melon. Unlike a human hand, it had three fingers, which might be more properly described as claws. Exactly the same disposition of fingers a man might have, in fact, if a man held his middle finger and forefinger, and his little and ring finger, together, and spread the two groups of fingers apart. A roof of steel slammed down from heaven. The boy felt warm blood spray over his back.

Then the sunlight returned to the sand, though the sand was now red rather than brown, and the gunman's headless body toppled to the ground in front of him. The man had not simply been decapitated. His head no longer existed. It had been squashed flat.

Beside him, his mother, still alive, was trembling. Looking at the front of her skirts, the boy realized suddenly that she had wet herself.

One of the Guardian's massive treads rose from the ground and whined over his head. For some reason the sole of its left foot was stenciled LEFT LEG, and that on its right foot was labeled RIGHT LEG. Arms fire both small and large whined and caromed off its carapace; the Guardian ignored it. It was moving out of the village, eastward, in the direction of the mining company army camped beyond the outskirts. Soon it was out of shooting range, but the boy could still hear guns going off around him. Single shot firearms! The villagers had brought out their antique home defense weapons and were using them on their oppressors. The boy swelled with pride.

Despite the fact that she had clearly wet herself, the boy's mother hauled herself to her feet, and remarked:

"The old fool! What does he think he's doing? At his age!"

The boy hopped up onto a ladder fixed to the main water tower. The Guardian was striding eastward like a force of nature, silhouetted by things exploding against it. The boy saw it pick a thing up from the ground, and hurl it like a discus. The thing was a light armored vehicle. He saw men tumble from it as it flew.

The mining company men were now flocking round a larger vehicle that was evidently their Big Gun. Most probably it had been brought in specially to deal with the possibility that the villagers might be able to revive their Guardian. It appeared to be a form of missile launcher, and the missile it fired looked frighteningly large. The turret on the top of the vehicle was being rotated round to bear on the approaching threat, and men were clearing from the danger space behind it.

The Guardian had stopped. Its hand was held before it, the elbow crooked, extended out towards the launcher. If had it been human, the boy would have described the posture it had now moved into as a defensive stance.

The boy blinked.

No. Surely not—

The missile blazed from its mounting, and then became invisible; and the Guardian's arm blurred with it.

Then the missile was tumbling away into the sky, its gyros trying frantically to put it back on course, wobbling unsteadily overhead; and the Guardian was standing in exactly the same position as before. A streak of rocket exhaust had licked up its arm and blackened its fingers.

The Guardian had brushed aside the missile in mid-air, so softly as not to detonate its fuse.

Men in the mining company launcher were standing staring motionless, as if their own operators had left them via their back entrances. The boy, however, suspected that other substances were currently leaving them by that exit; and as soon as the Guardian cranked into a forward stride again, the men began to run. By the time the Guardian eventually arrived at the launcher and methodically and thoroughly destroyed it, the boy was quite certain there were no human beings inside it. To the east of the village, he heard the terrific impact of the anti-armour missile eventually reaching its maximum range and aborting.

Then there was nothing on the face of the desert but running men, and smoking metal, and the gigantic figure of the Guardian standing casting a long, long shadow in the dawn.

The old man climbed down slowly, with painstaking exactness, just as he did in all things. He was breathing quite heavily by the time he swung off the last rung and into a crowd of cheering children.

"I knew Khan would not let us down," said Mother Tho.

"Khan Senior is a terrible fruit farmer," observed Father Magnusson, "but a Guardian operator without equal."

"His oranges are scabby-skinned and dry inside," agreed Mother Dingiswayo.

"All the same, I knew," opined Mother Jayaraman, "that he would eventually come in useful for something."

The old man shook his fist at the boy's father in mock rage. "Khan Junior! What a fool to expose yourself so! Do you want your family to grow up without a father?"

Khan grinned. "I am sorry, father. I have no idea what came over me."

"Maybe it is a hereditary condition," muttered the boy's mother.

"Well," said the old man, "at least it has turned out for the best. Had you not jumped out when you did, I might not have made it to the access ladder. One might almost imagine that that was your deliberate intention."

"I apologize if I did badly, father," said Khan. "I am more of a farmer by trade."

The old man walked across the square, to a handcart one of the younger boys had led out. In a fit of patriotic Commonwealther fervor, Father Magnusson had donated a hundred kilos of potatoes for a celebration, and they had been stacked in a neat pile ready for baking.

The old man picked one up, raw, and bit into it.

"Never apologize for being a farmer," said the old man, chewing gamely for a man with few remaining teeth. "After all, a gun will protect your family's life only once in a lifetime. But a potato," he said, gesturing with the tuber to illustrate his point, "is useful *every* day."

First published in *The Solaris Book of New Science Fiction: Volume Two*, edited by George Mann.

ABOUT THE AUTHOR

British writer **Dominic Green's** output has to date been confined almost entirely to the pages of *Interzone,* but he's appeared there a lot, selling them eighteen stories in the course of the last few years, although his story reprinted here appeared not in *Interzone* but in *The Solaris Book of Science Fiction 2.* Green lives in Northampton, England, where he works in information technology and teaches kung fu part time. On his website, the text of several unpublished novels and short stories can be found.

Realms of Dark, Deep and Cold
JULIE NOVAKOVA

These places never see sunlight, are buried deep under thick ice crusts and warmed mostly by radioactive decay and tidal forces: subsurface oceans of celestial objects far from their stars—if they have any. Decades ago, they were the domain of science fiction, until such places were hypothesized in our solar system thanks in part to *Voyager* flybys of Europa in 1979. Shortly after, the idea was popularized when it appeared in Arthur C. Clarke's *Space Odyssey* saga. Since then, we learned much more about characteristics of possible subsurface oceans, discovered that they probably exist on more worlds than we dared to expect just a few years ago, and that they're more fascinating than even SF authors hoped.

1979 changed our view of Europa forever. Images sent by the *Voyagers* sparked great interest in the moon. The surface was peculiar: quite smooth, with high albedo, few impact craters and a lot of strange ridges and cracks. This led to speculations about the existence of an ocean of liquid water under the outer ice shell. This would enable geological activity strong enough to erase older features like impact craters and provide extensional stress on the crust, resulting in formation of linear troughs we see on the surface.

Later, observations were able to tell us that these notions are most likely true. An ocean is the simplest explanation for the diverse geology of Europa's surface. Some of the present chemical compounds, couple with the interaction of the moon with Jupiter's magnetosphere indicates presence of liquid water underneath the ice layer. In the giant's magnetic field, Europa produces an induced magnetic field that would not be possible without a layer capable of conducting electrical current. The strength and direction of the induced field suggests an ocean of liquid water with a high concentration of dissolved salts and acids, at least a couple of dozen or more than 150 km deep.

These findings kindled a lot of enthusiasm about Europa, and lander missions were proposed. So why aren't we there already?

Besides worries about contamination, there is a serious technical problem. Jupiter's strong magnetic field interacts with particles around the planet (mainly released from Io's numerous volcanoes) and creates strong radiation belts full of accelerated ionized atoms and molecules. They caused *Pioneer 11* to lose the majority of images it had captured of Io. Even the probe *Galileo,* constructed to withstand the harsh environment close to Jupiter, experienced glitches due to the radiation.

Unfortunately for our plans of space exploration, Europa is right inside the belts. Any spacecraft to land there would have to endure extreme levels of ionizing radiation that would kill a human, even equipped with a space suit, in less than an hour. Sorry, Arthur C. Clarke, but astronauts walking on the surface of Europa shall remain science fiction.

Another problem for any missions to explore Europa's oceans directly is that we don't know the thickness and structure of the outer ice crust. Should we expect it to be just a few or several dozen kilometers thick, formed by hard brittle ice only or with additional warm convecting layer underneath? And if a device tried to melt through the shell, wouldn't it quickly become encrusted in salts and trapped?

So far, ESA's JUICE mission is planned to be launched in 2022 and to explore Ganymede, Callisto and Europa. All lander missions are still just concepts and will likely remain so for a long time, until we know more about the ice shell and the ocean.

Until the new spacecraft is able to tell us more, we can only speculate about the characteristics of Europa's ocean. Let's take a closer look on whether it could potentially support life as we know it.

Life needs a few basic things to exist: water as a solvent, an energy source, building blocks, chemical and energetic disequilibria. All of that can be found on Europa—but whether they are in sufficient quantities, we don't yet know.

Liquid water is not a constraint—even in the case of a very thick ice shell, there's most likely at least two times more than in the Earth's oceans. But water alone is not enough—any life would need chemical cycles to emerge. Without them, some substances could quickly become depleted or too abundant. The ocean also needs to be in contact with the rocky mantle for geochemical cycles to exist. According to most models, it is; but some predict a layer of high-pressure ice beneath the liquid, which would restrain access of water to the rock underneath. If material leaches from the bedrock into the water, the essential building blocks for life should be evident. Their concentration would likely be low, however, but many Earth extremophile microbes can cope with that.

The salinity and composition of the ocean remains another unresolved question. Based on the induced magnetic field and chemical compounds on the icy surface, it can be slightly less salty than Earth's ocean water or in contrast, almost twice as salty as the Dead Sea. In the latter case, only the most extreme halophile bacteria could survive such conditions.

Saltiness might not be the biggest problem. Imagine an ocean full of hydrolyzed sulfuric acid, with a pH less than 1. That's one extreme—but it can be highly alkaline as well. It can also be relatively reduced or oxidized, depending mostly on Europa's early history. Jupiter used to be warmer in the early days of the solar system and Europa could have had an ocean on the surface and an atmosphere of mostly water vapor. In such a case, the ocean would likely become oxidized.

As for temperature, it can be somewhere between a few °C above zero and -40 °C—still liquid thanks to high salinity and the anti-freeze effect of ammonia. Near hydrothermal vents, should there be any, the temperature could rise to a couple of hundred °C.

Organisms on Europa would also need to be able to withstand high pressure. On Earth, microorganisms capable of reproducing under extremes of all the above conditions together exist, many of them in the genus *Halomonas*. And with enough oxygen—which could be produced by breakdown of water by radiation occurring in the ice shell and absorbed into the ocean—even more microorganisms might possibly survive there.

How would possible Europan life gain energy? Methanogenesis, which can occur under a wide range of conditions feasible in the ocean, seems the most likely candidate so far. Depending on the real parameters, a Europan ocean might be capable of supporting several trophic levels and therefore a sustainable, albeit probably poor, ecosystem.

Europa is the most famous object with a probable inner ocean—but only one of many. Other two Galilean moons, Ganymede and Callisto, are also believed to host a subsurface body of liquid water. However, most models suggest that their oceans are "sandwiched" between the outer shell and a layer of high-pressure ice beneath. Without a direct connection with a rocky mantle, they would lack conditions for life that Europa might potentially harbor.

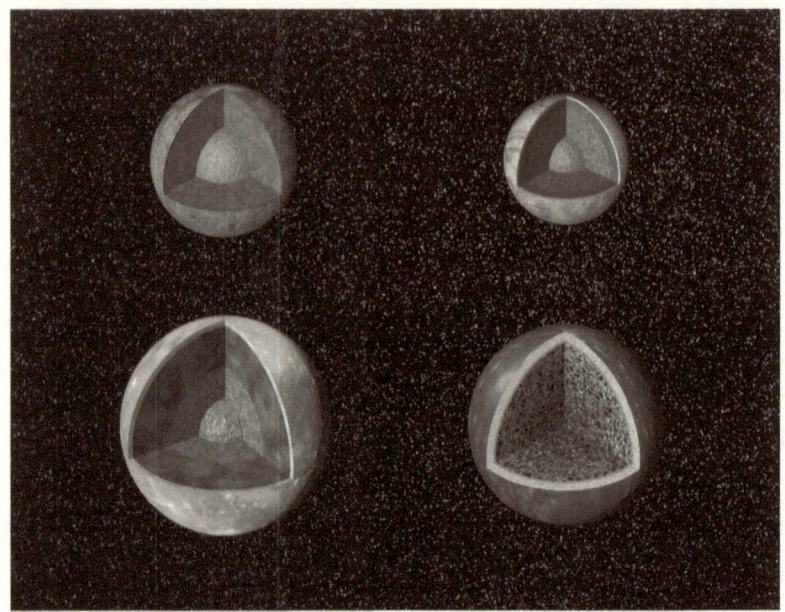

Image 1: The four Galilean moons. Europa, Ganymede and Callisto are all thought to have subsurface oceans. However, in Ganymede's case a thick layer of high-pressure ice beneath it is predicted. In Callisto's case, this layer is believed to be much thinner, but note that the moon's interior is not differentiated, unlike the other Galilean moons. As far as we can tell from gravitational pull data, it's a relatively uniform mixture of rock and ice. Unlike bedrock of a differentiated mantle, it wouldn't provide many opportunities of geochemical cycles and any hydrothermal activity is highly unlikely. Courtesy of NASA/JPL-Caltech.

If we move from Jupiter to Saturn, we'll encounter one of the most intriguing bodies of the solar system: Titan. Under the orange-brownish haze of its dense atmosphere, there are alkane seas and rivers, tholin dunes and methane snows. About two hundred km underneath this fantastic landscape, an ocean of water and ammonia might be hidden. But according to most models, it's trapped between two layers of ice as well.

Another fascinating object orbiting Saturn is the tiny moon Enceladus. Ever since the *Cassini* spacecraft observed geysers on its south pole, its cryovolcanic activity remains a mystery. Current tidal heating of the moon is negligible, and so should be the amount of radioactive decay due to its small size. Models of radioactive heating failed to explain the ocean—yet the moon is *very* active. Its surface appears young and long linear "tiger stripes" near the south pole indicate extensional stress: an indirect sign of subsurface liquid. More intense past tidal forces and present shear heating have been proposed but it's still not certain whether they'd be sufficient for keeping the little moon spawning ice particles into Saturn's previously mysterious E-ring. Most models suggest a large pocket of water underneath the south pole but a global ocean is not ruled out. What's more, it's likely in contact with bedrock and many authors agree that the geochemical conditions for life might be met.

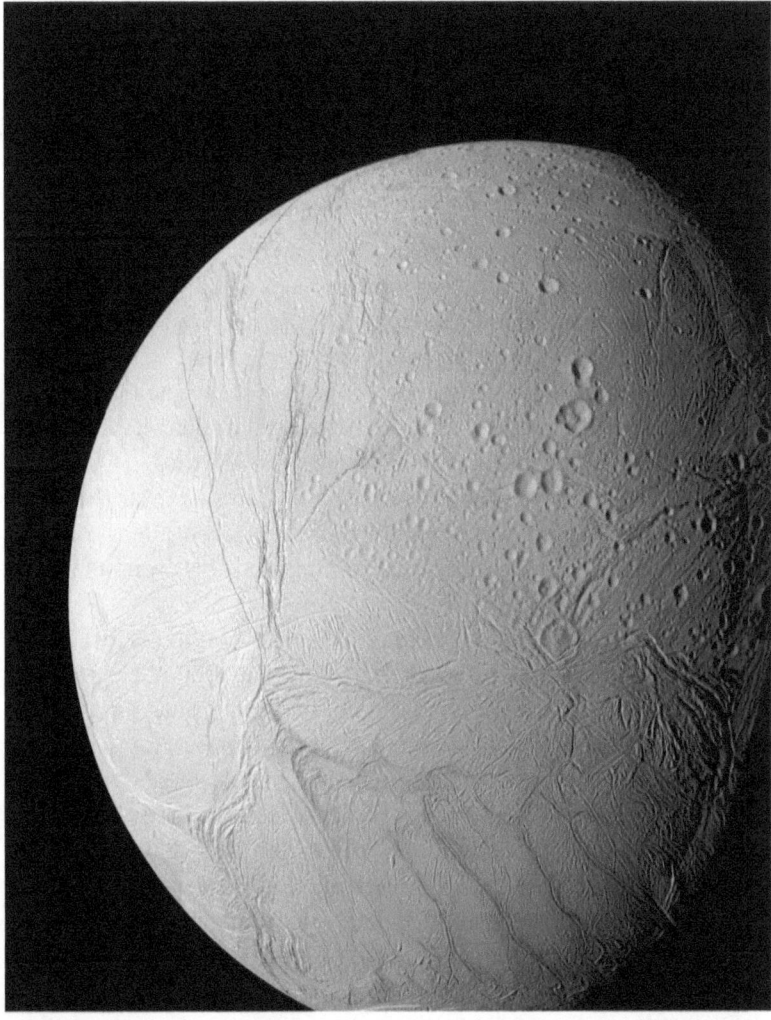

Image 2: A false-color mosaic of pictures of Enceladus taken by the Cassini spacecraft. The famous "tiger stripes" can be seen near the south pole where geysers were also observed. Courtesy of NASA/JPL/Space Science Institute.

Existence of a subsurface ocean is also feasible on several other Saturn's moons: Dione, where water vapor was recently detected, and Rhea; less likely Tethys and Iapetus.

Similar claims were made about Titania and Oberon, the largest moons of the ice giant Uranus. But for an example of a truly cryovolcanically active body, we need to move even further: to Neptune and its only large satellite, Triton. Triton is thought to be a captured Kuiper belt object due to its retrograde orbit, high tilt and the conspicuous absence of other large moons. It's theorized that Triton might have "kicked them out" in the wild early days of being caught by Neptune's gravity.

Plumes of water have been detected on Triton and its surface tells a similar story to that of Europa or Enceladus. During the early epoch of the solar system, tidal heating of the captured moon would be significant, enough to melt a part of its icy interior. These oceans, covered by a shell that doesn't conduct heat particularly well, might have a long duration. Combined with radioactive decay and enough anti-freeze compounds like ammonia, plentiful in these regions of the solar system, we can see that it's likely not easy to freeze an ocean once it's there.

But we need not to be constrained to moons of the giants. If we look closer, in the space between orbits of Mars and Jupiter, we find a wide asteroid belt. Could bodies of liquid water be there too?

Just recently, water vapor was detected on Ceres—the largest object of the belt, containing about one third of the mass of the whole belt. The spacecraft *Dawn* is scheduled to arrive to the dwarf planet in February 2015.

However, the asteroid belt between Mars and Jupiter is just a playground compared to the Kuiper belt. Beyond the orbit of Neptune lies an area where our Sun appears as a mere very bright star, and countless worlds of ice take their long journeys around it. The best known Kuiper belt object is the dwarf planet Pluto, with its faithful companion Charon. When the probe *New Horizons* was launched, Pluto was still considered a planet, but was reclassified shortly thereafter. This changed nothing about the fact that Pluto is an interesting and mysterious object. No close observations have been made yet—but that's about to change in 2015 when *New Horizons* should reach Pluto, its large moon Charon and four smaller moons.

During the flyby, it might tell us more fascinating facts about Pluto than expected. In 2006, shortly after the probe was launched, a study by Hussmann et al. explored the topic of radiogenic heating of mid-sized icy objects. They found that most models permitted the existence of a subsurface liquid body of water not just in Pluto and Charon, but also a number of other Kuiper belt objects. If an ocean truly is inside Pluto, no fossil bulge from an early period of faster rotation should exist—the influence of the ocean would erase it. Observation of cryovolcanism—indicated on Charon by the spectroscopic detection of crystalline water ice—would be an even better proof. Next year, we shall see.

Eris, a dwarf planet discovered in 2005, might be an even better candidate for an ocean under ice than Pluto due to its larger size and therefore more radioactive elements. The list of Kuiper belt objects likely to host subsurface liquid water might also continue to grow including bodies like Quaoar and Orcus.

The furthest object of the solar system, for which a subsurface ocean has been proposed, is the dwarf planet Sedna. In its perihelion, the point of the least distance to the Sun, it's 76 AU away from our star—still more than twice and half further than Pluto in its own perihelion. However, due to the extremely high eccentricity of its orbit, Sedna travels as far as about 940 AU far from the Sun in the aphelion—much more than seven times the distance *Voyager 1*, the furthest human-made object, has made until now. Like Triton, it can tell us a wild fascinating story about the origins of our solar system—if we listen.

It's hard to imagine that oceans of liquid water would exist so very far from the Sun but models of radioactive decay suggest it's possible. And with enough ammonia and a well-isolating shell, even an ocean with temperature around -100 °C might exist.

Sedna is just one of the solar system objects that proved that our own system is more fantastic and its history more compelling than we could imagine. But our gaze inevitably travels to other stars as we ask ourselves a question whether conditions suitable for life exist *out there.*

Existences of subsurface oceans have been proposed for several known exoplanets, namely three planets in the Gliese 667 C system (f, e and d) and Gliese 581d. Will we ever find out whether these predictions are true?

Detection of subsurface oceans on extrasolar planets would be complicated—but nevertheless feasible. We can use the same indicators of cryovolcanism as for the objects orbiting our Sun: crystalline water ice and ammonia hydrate. They can be detected spectroscopically, hopefully by the next generation of telescopes like proposed FINESSE, ESM, EchO and last but not least the JWST, planned to be launched in 2018.

But should we constrain ourselves just to looking to other stars?

We've already discovered a couple of starless, rogue planets. Some may have been ejected from their birth systems, and some may have formed on their own in case of brown dwarfs. Some may host subsurface oceans under thick crusts of ice; some may have exomoons with such conditions.

There are at least one hundred billion stars in our galaxy. Many of these systems could be homes for objects with subsurface oceans; we need not look just into narrow "habitable zones" for such places. And according to the more optimistic estimates, there can be twice as many free-floating planets than there are stars in the Milky Way.

Though most subsurface oceans would probably have trouble supporting even extremophile life forms as we know them, they still may be one of the most abundant environments potentially suitable for life. Looking at our own solar system and beyond, we can see countless worlds full of the most intriguing possibilities.

> " 'Oceans under ice' could be a common feature . . . , largely spread around low-mass stars in the Galaxy."
> —Ehrenreich & Cassan, 2006

Special thanks to Tomas Petrasek, Czech author of astrobiology popular science books "Vzdalene svety I, II" ("Distant Worlds I and II"), for beta-reading the article.

ABOUT THE AUTHOR

Julie Novakova was born in 1991 in Prague, the Czech Republic. She works as a writer and an evolutionary biologist. So far, she has published three novels, some twenty short stories in Czech and one other story in English (*The Brass City in Penny Dread Tales Vol. Three: In Darkness Clockwork Shine*). Her novels were *The Crime on The Poseidon City (Zlocin na Poseidon City)*, *Never Trust Anything (Nikdy never nicemu)* and *A Silent Planet (Ticha planeta)*. Julie's short stories appeared in Czech speculative fiction magazines (*Ikarie*, *XB-1* and *Pevnost*) and anthologies. She's a severe were-workaholic (which means that most of the time she's quite lazy and she magically transforms the night before deadline).

The Blue Collar Craftsman
& the Salesmen on Mars:
A Conversation with Ben Tanzer

JEREMY L. C. JONES

Orphans by Ben Tanzer opens with Norrin Radd staring in a mirror. Tanzer isn't soft-peddling a fiction workshop cliche, here. Pock-marked and shadow-boxing, Radd is pure Willie Loman from *Death of a Salesman*-meets-Rick Deckard of *Bladerunner.*

"Always be closing!"

Radd's working himself up. Or he's trying to, at least.

"Always be closing!"

He needs work. He needs this job. He's broke. He's got a family—a wife, a child. His life is "fraught with anger, pain and frustration" and "sporadic bursts of joy and peace and love."

Earth is dismal. Baidu, formerly Chicago, is no garden of Eden. It's not too hellish if you have a job. The homeless live in camps on the lakefront. Drones hover about making sure everyone stays where they belong.

There are echoes of Philip K. Dick, and flashes of Bradbury, Vonnegut, and Herman Melville's "Bartleby, the Scrivener: A Story of Wall Street."

Remember Bartleby and his "I would prefer not to"?

But these influences strobe, add color. Tanzer doesn't linger too long, doesn't lean too hard on his favorites. This is very much his book—a sometimes quietly beautiful, sometimes terrifyingly raw scream of desperation.

The first twenty pages of *Orphans* is gritty and depressing and hard to look away from.

Will space live up to Radd's dreams? Will it solve all his problems or just cause more?

No simple answers here.

And there shouldn't be. This guy's too good a writer for that.

Tanzer is the author of *My Father's House, You Can Make Him Like You, 99 Problems,* and *Lost in Space.* When he's not out running the streets of Chicago, he's the director of publicity and content strategy at Curbside Splendor Publishing and blogs at This Blog Will Change Your Life.

What do you enjoy about writing fiction in general and speculative fiction in particular?

The most immediate thing for me is that I'm not limited to my experiences or even my own fantasies. Fiction allows, even encourages, me to step outside my own head. I think one of the great challenges for any author is writing their way through, and out of, their own life, and what they know, sloughing off their own stories and fears and joys and finding out what else is out there they can write about. Fiction provides a bridge for accomplishing this. Or, attacking it anyway. Speculative fiction then furthers this opportunity for me in two ways. First, I am writing about worlds that don't quite exist as I know them. They need to read like something both familiar, and yet not, just close enough to be known, or familiar, without being close enough, and so you need to stretch beyond the known, or the known known, as one former Defense Secretary who shall go unnamed might have said. So, yes, we all know what the space shuttle is, and that the space shuttles have been retired, but do we know anyone who takes one to work? And second, I have no natural connection to, or filter for, writing stories that are surreal or bizzarro, but that limits the possibilities of where the realistic fiction I want to write can go. Speculative fiction, which makes more sense to me, gives me that platform though. A robot in a surreal tale of husband and wife in a marriage gone wrong doesn't translate for me as a writer, but a robot doorman and guide, I can see that, and I can write it.

Where did *Orphans* start for you?

I was out running and had this idea that I wanted to do something about a father and a son and that the father would be a salesman. I thought it could be a sort of homage to *Death of a Salesman,* because why aim low, right? But then I thought, maybe it shouldn't be quite so contemporary, and maybe I should focus on trying not to repeat myself. So I thought, what if the father sold real estate on Mars, and then maybe it could be more of a mash-up of the *Martian Chronicles* and *Glengarry Glen Ross?* With his obligations to his family, he had little choice about whether to take the job? Maybe then, I could also go for a Silver Surfer vibe? And what if work in general is not really available at all anyway, but it feels like the only job available to him at all? If the near future could look like that, then the protagonist could also fly in retired space shuttles to work, have a clone replace him at home while traveling for work, and even be offered the occasional robot hand job for doing his job well.

Your dad was a painter, right? How much did his work influence you—the work itself or his creative process?

He was, and his work, and his presence, looms over this book, and much of what I've written. There is the dynamic of work and how the need for work can warp what families need from the worker. My father was a great dad, and a great artist, but he was also clearly conflicted by how much the family needed of him, and how this impacted his ability to embrace the selfishness any artist needs to be successful. On the other hand, because I watched him struggle to achieve the success he hoped for, I don't doubt for a moment that I have fought being wholly immersed in the artist's life, and in fact have always striven to have 9-5 jobs with steady paychecks, health insurance, and all the things one needs to feel stable and take care of their family. And all of that tension is built into the lead character Norrin's anxieties as well. Finally, and connectedly, I hope, and think, is my approach to this book and anything I work on. My dad was a blue collar, craftsman, artist, who believed artists were born with a gift, but had to roll-up their sleeves and do the hard work required to be successful. I have tried to model that. I try to never be precious about time or the place I write, or search for the right music or mood, and I never wait for inspiration. I just try to work everyday, make the time, be in the moment, and seek perfection in all its messy grandiosity.

Was it fun pushing Chicago into the future, handing it over to the Corporation, and allowing it to decay around the edges?

It was fun. I should acknowledge that I tend to be more interested in the landscape inside people's heads and how those landscapes may be decaying around the edges, but this was a lot of fun, and the threads I tried to think about in changing Chicago into Baidu were several-fold. First, if the focus is on a city that is slowly being turned into a police state, what might that look like? How would the police act and how would the citizens be controlled? So, there are helicopters endlessly moving people along, because there can be no chaos or group activity allowed. And if that same city had mortgaged its future and naming rights to some unknowable corporation and other countries such as China, what impact does that have on the culture? So, in this case for example, people constantly protest the city's name change in the former Daley Plaza, in the same way they protested Marshall Fields becoming Macy's.

Further, if there is no work, and no future, what does that look like? That looks in part like young people forming flash mobs to taunt the Corporation and the police that represent them. I was also influenced though by reading about this social norm in Japan where men who lose their jobs still dress in their suits, leave the house as if going to work, and then sit in the park, before returning home at dinner time like they've been at work all day. And so in Baidu, unemployed men wander the streets in their old suits searching for work.

Finally, I played with ideas I had about Chicago that have some pop culture or literary relevance, so for example, the salesmen of *Glengarry Glen Ross* appear as co-workers of Norrin's, and he and his wife Shalla hung out on Belmont at the Dunkin' Donuts when they were young punks, and that latter reference is based on reality, but also as an homage to the young punks in *American Skin* by Don DeGrazia, one of the great recent novels about an already different Chicago that's fading into history.

***I read somewhere that your early fiction was very autobiographical
and that got you into writing non-fiction. So, how much of Norrin
Radd is based on you?***

I had this idea about *Orphans,* how it was going to be this rumination
on fathers and sons, the intersection of family and work, and all things
science fictional, *Martian Chronicles,* Silver Surfer and such. And I
was going along and writing it, and loving it, and then one weekend I
had to fly to California to co-keynote a conference for my day job. We
were in the middle of some challenges at home and it felt like it was a
terrible time to leave. But I left, and when I called my wife from Las
Vegas where I had a layover, she sounded tired, still strong, but beat-up,
and as I sat there, I asked myself why I thought it had been okay to go
on this trip at all.

It was something my boss had asked me to do, and canceling would
have been embarrassing for me at the organization, but did I really
have to go? And did I have to say yes when my boss asked me to do so?
When, and where, can we say "I prefer not to," or "I can't," and if you
can ask yourself that question, then maybe you have to ask yourself
how much of this is also about your own ego, and need for escape and
affirmation? This crept into the book, and that is how I'm like Norrin
Radd. He is doing what he believes he has to do without ever quite
asking whether he has to do it, or if there is another way.

Further, he is good at what he does, and he needs the affirmation
that comes with doing well, and I am like that too. We both have issues
with ego and neediness. We also though, both worry about hurting
those we love, even when we know they are strong enough to handle
what they need to deal with. Finally, we both know what it's like to
feel trapped, and not because of marriage itself, because we are both
married to people we love, or by having children, because we both have
children we want to devour, but by the expectations that comes with
those roles, both real and imagined.

***What were some of the surprises for you along the way while
writing the novel?***

I don't map my books out in great detail anyway, but I always know
where the story is going, and where it will end. Yet, there is a scene late
in the book where the protagonist is thinking of confronting his clone,
or Terrax, and reminisces about an accident his son had. In that scene
which I hadn't totally thought through beforehand, I had no plans to

write about an accident, much less channel an accident my own son had, but there it was, it seemed perfect, and I ran with it.

The other kind of surprises though seem more self-serving to me, but there were ideas that I fixated on while writing that I didn't necessarily have a reference point for, but have since become a more pronounced part of the news and culture. I had read an article in the *Nation* somewhere along the way about how the top one percent of the population possesses something like ninety percent of the nation's wealth, which at the time was still a newer reality, and so I referred to these members of society in *Orphans* as "1-Percenters." This was before the term "the 99 percent" had any traction however. Further, the idea to write about flash mobs protesting the Corporation emerged from a conversation I had with a writer friend of mine, but that conversation was long before Occupy Wall Street.

The characters in the book are also aware that someone, somewhere, is constantly listening to everything they say, and that is something that felt "near future" to me, but even then I cut some of that out so as to not seem too out there. Of course since then, all of the stories about the NSA have come out and now I realize I couldn't have been excessive enough.

Which, if any, of the reviews of and comments about *Orphans* have baffled you? Have any of them been really far out there?

One comment was focused on whether we need another dystopic story set in Chicago. Which is a good question. I had never heard of *Divergent* when I first started *Orphans,* though I have since read it and really enjoyed it. I think we have room for multiple stories set here, though I also wonder if the need for Chicago authors to write those stories says something about what it means to actually live here.

Differently though, two reviews commented on the role of family in the book which did catch me off-guard. One review, which was generally positive, implied that I was suggesting that the creation and maintenance of traditional families is of the highest import. I don't think I meant to imply that, nor do I think I remotely feel like that, but I do need to think about that now.

Somewhat similarly, another review suggested that since the protagonist is conflicted about being away from his wife so he can provide for the family, and she is unhappy that he has to, I was in essence suggesting that future looks like the 1950's, but with space travel. Again, I don't think I intended that, but I definitely need to think about it now.

So arguably, nothing too out there, sadly, because that would be fun, though there is now an endless need for self-examination looming in my own near future for sure.

Also, I'm curious as to whether you think University of Chicago has shaped your thinking in a significant way? Seems to me that that place trains minds in a very specific way of thinking.

I went to University of Chicago for graduate school in social work. I had been out of school for several years and I hadn't started attempting to be a writer yet. I had done very well on written assignments throughout high school, where I didn't do well otherwise, and college, where I did. I say all that because I assumed I would be up to the task of writing good, thoughtful papers in graduate school as well. But I wasn't. I was terrible, and I couldn't figure out how to get untracked for most of the first quarter.

One of my professors that quarter suggested I take an extracurricular undergraduate writing workshop called the Little Red Schoolhouse and I was offended by the suggestion. Why I was offended seems ridiculous to me now, but there is that whole ego thing. Anyway, I took the course my second year because I had a thesis I had to write, and the experience was transformative for me. I still hadn't started writing yet outside of school work, and I wouldn't for some time, but all of the endless best practices I learned in that workshop I still use today. For example, what you write always makes sense in your head, but that doesn't mean it will to anyone else, which is why you have to let other people read your drafts.

This is basic stuff for most writers I'm sure, but it was new to me, and nothing I had ever thought about before The best thing I learned though, was don't edit a first draft until you are entirely done with it, and I still apply that rule to everything from essays to novels, no pause, no looking back, no getting stuck, just keep going until you're done. Which has served me really well, despite the ten years of student loans I had to pay-off to learn these lessons in the first place.

You've mentioned some of the inspirations for and influences on this book. Could you go into a little more detail about some of the speculative fiction that inspired and inspires you?

I'm glad you asked, and not because these inspirations necessarily directly influenced this book, but because there's so much speculative fiction I love, especially when I was younger and these books were so wonderfully, and necessarily, escapist for me. So, along with *The Martian Chronicles,* there is also Bradbury's *The Illustrated Man,* which was very popular in my house because my father was also a tattoo artist for a time. The John Carter Warlord of Mars series by Edgar Rice Burroughs was huge. I read those books again and again, and I loved some of the more obscure Burroughs pulp fiction as well, for example *The Mucker* and *Pellucidar.* Later when I was in college I had the opportunity to take a science fiction class and got to read The Foundation Trilogy by Asimov for the first time, which just crushed me, and *Dune,* though I'm, not sure how I got so far not reading it, *The Handmaiden's Tale,* which was so beautiful and horrible. I also think some of Vonnegut, who I consumed voraciously too, certainly qualifies, say *Cat's Cradle* for example. Recently, someone was kind of enough to compare *Orphans* to *How to Live Safely in a Science Fictional Universe* by Charles Yu, which I hadn't read, but since have, and it was terrific, just so knowing and smart. A friend of mine, Peter Tieryas Liu, just had his novel *Bald New World,* come out, and I'm just into it, but it's terrific as well. Beyond the literary though, I should definitely give a shout-out to *The Twilight Zone,* which I was obsessive about, *Logan's Run, Escape from New York, Star Wars,* and *Blade Runner,* which just blew me away, and unlike some of these other loves of mine, certainly had a tonal impact on *Orphans.*

What's next for this world and these people and you as a writer?

This is grandiose of me, possibly obnoxious, you be the judge, but I always saw *Orphans* as a trilogy of sorts, where the first book would be from the father's perspective, the second from the mother's, and the third from the son's. And so I have started working on a sequel titled *Foundlings* written from Shalla's point of view and right now it's got a road trip vibe, and is feeling like a mash-up of the *Wizard of Oz* and the *Odyssey,* but with robots and clones and time travel. We'll see. I also have a novel titled *Ballad* I'm working on about teenage girl drug dealer and alien abduction. And I'm thrilled to let you know that I just had an essay collection come out which I focused on fatherhood as viewed through the lens of *Star Wars, NAS, Mad Men,* Patrick Ewing, and Vanilla Ice, among other things. It's titled *Lost in Space,* and I think that everyone may just want to buy it right now, well *Lost in Space,* and *Orphans,* both. Is that a selfish request?

ABOUT THE AUTHOR

Jeremy L. C. Jones is a freelance writer, editor, and teacher. He is the Staff Interviewer for *Clarkesworld Magazine* and a frequent contributor to *Kobold Quarterly* and *Booklifenow.com*. He teaches at Wofford College and Montessori Academy in Spartanburg, SC. He is also the director of Shared Worlds, a creative writing and world-building camp for teenagers that he and Jeff VanderMeer designed in 2006. Jones lives in Upstate South Carolina with his wife, daughter, and flying poodle.

Another Word: Killing Rage

DANIEL ABRAHAM

I'm not telling anybody what they should do.

I'm guessing that since you're here reading essays on *Clarkesworld,* you're most likely a fan of genre fiction and maybe spend a little time on the Internet. Seems pretty safe as assumptions go. And because of that, you're probably aware of the conflicts that have been troubling the online community of fans and professionals recently: Toni Weisskopf's essay on fandom and John Scalzi's response, Jonathan Ross hosting the Hugo Awards, Sean Fodera's comments on Mary Robinette Kowal, Truesdale's petition about the SFWA Bulletin, Wiscon's disinvitation Elizabeth Moon, Racefail '09.

The list goes on, I am reliably informed, back through Silverberg's famous insistence that James Tiptree Jr. couldn't possibly be a woman, Ballard and Moorcock's advancement of the New Wave, and pretty much everything Harlan Ellison's ever done until it disappears in the mists of history sometime before 1930.

This, for better or worse, is the water we swim in now, and probably always was before. As with everything else in our culture, the Internet has made it weirder and faster and more immediate and more anonymous. We've had lots of calls for civility, and lots of responses that those calls for civility usually mean you'd like the other person to shut up and stop bothering you. We've had a lot of reasoned, careful commentary by thoughtful people, and a lot of public venting of spleen. We've had people who genuinely wanted to come to some deeper understanding and accord, and some who seem to like lighting conversations on fire just to watch them burn.

Science fiction and fantasy—more than any other genre—has a

deep tradition of direct engagement of fans and writers. The narrative of fandom as community—almost as family—was around long before I came on the scene. Truth of the matter is, fandom can be a bruising place to be a professional and a fan. Maybe it's worse now than it was before, maybe it's only different. But it's left me thinking about conflict, rage, rhetorical violence, my experience with them, and the decisions I've made about who I want to be publically and professionally.

I'm going to say this again: I'm not telling anybody what they should do. I'm not interested in dictating how folks act or speak, what they should believe or how they should believe it. Not that I don't have opinions about that, but I'm not writing a sermon.

Right now, I'm just laying out part of what I think and how I got here, and what Marshall Rosenberg, bell hooks, and Marcus Aurelius have to do with it. If it's useful to you, that's great. If it's not, you'll maybe have another perspective on it. Or on me. That's fine too.

So there's this guy, JB. He's been a friend of mine since middle school, and has always been more spiritual and more religious—though that's not quite the right word for him—and more engaged with justice than I am. Turns out that's not actually a very high bar, but he clears it. His track record on recommending interesting, thought-provoking books is really good, and maybe a decade ago, maybe a little more than that, he pointed me toward an author named Marshall Rosenberg, and a book called *Nonviolent Communication*.

I can't express clearly enough how much I dislike this book. Not the content—which I'll get to in a minute—but the style. This is the most touchy-feely, Pollyanna, syrupy-sweet, Kumbaya-singing book I have ever pulled my self through by the eyelashes. It's got amateur rhyming poetry in it about people and their hearts. I'm not this guy. My skin crawled when I read this, as it has every time I've reread it since. (This, turns out, is a lot.) Because wrapped in this chalky candy heart of a book is a manual for how to invite—even insist on—conflict, and see it through until it's resolved.

It talks about withholding judgment, cultivating compassion, listening deeply (and how to include some error correction in that) all with the aim of having actual, meaningful communication happen. And the thing that was most revelatory to me in reading it was the analysis of how useful conflict happens in a range. We can avoid it by minimizing it—turning away, pretending there's not a problem—or by escalating out of it, derailing it into name calling and judgments.

If you had to pick a single book that has had the most effect on my public persona, this one's it. I grew up with insults and wit where other kids just hit each other. I have a very good toolbox when it comes to verbal violence—I'm kind of good at it. And we have a long and vibrant history of gadflies and bullies in our community. Engaging in that is tempting for me, not in the least because I'm pretty sure I could hold my own even in some pretty high weight classes. This is to say, I know I can escalate out of a conflict. I know I can tease people into a kind of semi-coherent rage. I've done it; we called it high school. And, from what I hear from my cohorts, part of college. It could have been my professional persona. But instead I got interested in this other set of tools, and this other way to have conflicts. Instead of being showy and witty and clever and outrageous, I got to dissect what the issues really are. It turns out that I like that better.

Rosenberg—like pretty much everyone who's been engaged with fandom in the last few years—had to talk about anger. Anger is the emotion most closely associated with violence. That's true for me, and I'm guessing it's true for you. And this is true to the point that the two often get confused. Expressions of anger often read like rhetorical violence, and criticisms of someone's rhetorical style are easy to confuse with (or conflate with or use as) telling the writer that their emotions are wrong. Rosenberg is utterly against violence in how we talk to each other. But he's strongly in favor of the complete, accurate, and uncompromising expression of anger.

I had to sit with that for a long time before I had any idea what he was talking about. It wasn't an easy thing for me to parse, and I still struggle with it sometimes. The good news is, I have an example I can go back to.

When I picked up the book *Killing Rage* by Dr. bell hooks, I thought that the title would be an essay about how to, y'know, kill rage. Get rid of it. Boy-howdy, did I have *that* wrong. The essay *Killing Rage* is about living in a state of justified anger, and as a piece of writing, it's a thing of beauty.

Full disclosure: I think bell hooks is one of the best thinkers we have about race, gender, violence, and punishment that we've got. That particular essay is a difficult, upsetting read. It's more than a description of anger; it's an expression of it. It gives the context for it, examples that explain and justify it, and a description of a bone-deep, powerful anger. She talks about the temptation to violence. She describes having violent, even murderous, fantasies.

And—here's why I will never stop admiring her—she never escalates out of the conflict. She never becomes easy to discount or put down. She expresses, even evokes, pain in a way that demands the reader stand witness to it. And she envisions moving it "beyond fruitless scapegoating of any group, linking it instead to a passion for freedom and justice that illuminates, heals, and makes redemptive struggle possible."

She gave me an example of the difference between anger and violence. This also seems like the right moment to mention it again: I'm not telling anybody what they should do.

I've also adopted Marcus Aurelius as one of my intellectual bodyguards. Here's this guy with the power of a god among men. He was the Emperor of the only superpower of his time. He was able to order anyone who offended him to die, able to order any woman he desired to his bed; a man in a position of almost no social restraint. Yet, when you read his meditations, it's like you're talking to someone who's been working in tech support too long.

Begin each day by telling yourself "Today I shall be meeting with interference, ingratitude, disloyalty, ill-will, and selfishness; all of them due to the offender's ignorance of what is good and what is evil." Or, another of my favorites, "The art of living is more like wrestling than dancing."

I'll go back to Marcus on the days where I need someone to remind me that people are just people—venal, selfish, immoral, mean-spirited, small—and that it isn't my problem. I have control over who I am, and over what I do, and if I can get that shit under control, I'm actually doing pretty well. When it comes to being in this community of professionals and amateurs and fans, where we are hip deep in grievances both legitimate and bizarre, these three folks are my touchstones. They're who I've chosen to cultivate.

I would like the field to be more civil, so I'm going to be civil, even when I think I'd be justified not to. I would like the conversations we have to be more compassionate, so I'm going to try to exercise compassion when I'm talking to folks, even when I think they're full of shit. When I'm angry about something, I'll try to express that completely and fully and while keeping my temper. When someone's angry with me, I'll try to listen past my defensiveness to what they're saying, whether I agree with them or not. When I think someone is arguing with me in bad faith, I'm going to walk away.

I'd like our conflicts about ideology, politics, and religion to be less violent, so I'm trying to be less violent when I talk about them. On the days I can't bring myself to that, I stay off the Internet.

I would like my field to respect the quality of work more than the skin tone or sexual preferences of the author who wrote it, so I try to celebrate good work by folks who I think deserve more attention than they've gotten. I try to tack against the parts of mainstream culture that I think are crap, and hopefully I get it right more than I screw it up.

I'm trying to become the change I want to see in the field; more professional, thoughtful, compassionate, non-violent, and open to conflict and change.

And part of that? I'm not telling anybody what they should do.

ABOUT THE AUTHOR

Daniel Abraham is a writer of genre fiction with a dozen books in print and over thirty published short stories. His work has been nominated for the Nebula, World Fantasy, and Hugo Awards and has been awarded the International Horror Guild Award. He also writes as MLN Hanover and (with Ty Franck) as James S. A. Corey. He lives in the American Southwest.

Editor's Desk:
Supporting our Favorites
NEIL CLARKE

The nomination period for the Hugo Awards came to a close at the end of March. As has become tradition in recent years, many fans and professionals took to blogs and social media to either direct attention to their eligible works, make a case for their favorites, or remind you to vote. Yes, I am among those guilty of doing so.

We at *Clarkesworld* have been fortunate enough to win three Hugo Awards and I've been nominated twice for Best Editor Short Form. Last year's nominations and win were a very personal victory after a year highlighted by a heart attack and other medical issues. I can't possibly describe how much the show of support meant to me and I continue to hope the authors, artists and editors behind all of my favorite works are similarly celebrated someday. Unfortunately, that isn't likely. There will always be someone or something that you fell should have been recognized, but wasn't. It's the nature of awards.

That's where my mind went as I selected my nominations. In several cases, I agonized over who would get my top five votes. It simply wasn't possible to nominate everyone I thought deserved recognition. And yes, sometimes there isn't even a category (like anthology or magazine) to provide an opportunity to draw attention to a worthy project, but that's a discussion for another day.

I'm not sure why it took me so long to realize that I already have a reasonable way to recognize everyone I want to, even those without a category. It's even something that will help sales of their work, which sadly, isn't always true of awards. I'm a bit embarrassed, because it's an alternative I've suggested to people who wanted to support *Clarkesworld*: writing reviews at Amazon, Apple, B&N, etc. Your reviews of us have proved to me that they have value.

There are people for which this activity comes naturally. They can write up paragraphs and paragraphs about any book or story they have read. Fearless, they toss their words into the ether for all to see. Then there are people like me. I agonize over every word and have trouble clicking that save button. I think those of us in my group have been making things too difficult for ourselves. Why shouldn't we be satisfied writing "I read a lot of anthologies and this was the best one I read in 2013" and leaving it at that?

Short and sweet reviews have their value. They open the door to discussion and give weight to the reviews of our more eloquent friends. They boost the profile of the author and their work, and when these reviews are on retailers' site (Amazon, Apple, B&N, etc.), they have an actual impact on sales. Even adding to a pile of tens, hundreds, thousands, or more reviews has value because it isn't just about quantity, but also how recently they've been reviewed.

I know why I haven't been following my own advice. I was physically and verbally bullied as a child. I was also mocked for my taste in music and books for many years. We put up walls to protect ourselves and mine keep a lot of stuff private. I like to think that I'm doing much better these days. I blog, have a decent social media presence, participate on panels of give talks, but that's pretty much a construct I call "Work Neil" or "Con Neil." I'm never entirely relaxed, except among family or a handful of friends.

Since the heart attack, I've tried to take more of a "life is too short" attitude towards things. I'm forty-seven. I think it's long past time to get over this particular ingrained fear from my childhood. (It was either this one or fear of needles, which is a bit more complicated and painful.) Besides, this has the added benefit of helping people I respect.

This month, I will start posting reviews. I will take baby steps, starting with one-sentence reviews and working my way towards a whole paragraph. Since I want them to have successful careers where they actually make a living from their work (hey, it's my goal, so I should be supporting others in their efforts to do the same), I will emphasize reviewing on retail sites over my own blog. I might even be brave enough to post something on Goodreads.

So, who will join me on this adventure?

ABOUT THE AUTHOR

Neil Clarke is the editor of *Clarkesworld Magazine,* owner of Wyrm Publishing and a two-time Hugo Nominee for Best Editor (short form). He currently lives in NJ with his wife and two children.

About the Artist

PETER MOHRBACHER

Peter Mohrbacher is an independent illustrator and concept artist living in the Chicago area.

WEBSITE

www.vandalhigh.com